✥ SPARKS SHALL ✥
RISE

REAWAKENED FLAMES

LINDSAY
McCAFFERTY

❖ SPARKS SHALL ❖

RISE

REAWAKENED FLAMES

Content Warning

Content dealing with anxiety, health anxiety, depression, obsessive-compulsive disorder, and suicidal ideation.

Sparks Shall Rise: Reawakened Flames

© 2020, 2018 Lindsay McCafferty

This work of fiction is not a substitute for real advice from licensed physicians, therapists, or mental health professionals. Any portrayal of medical practices or therapy is fictitious and not to be interpreted as accurate.

The story, names, characters, and incidents portrayed in this production are from the author's imagination and are fictitious. No identification with actual persons (living or deceased), places, and events is intended or should be inferred.

Second Edition (2022)

Cover, Map, Logo & Title Pages designed by MiblArt

Interior formatting made using Atticus.

ISBN-13 (Paperback): 978-0-578-63084-7

authorlindsaymccafferty.com

PREFACE

I never expected that I would develop mental illness, let alone more than one type. My life up until that point could be defined as simply normal. This didn't mean I was immune. No one is. The mental illness began slowly and eventually took hold of me, sometimes leaving me almost completely crippled mentally.

I never expected to write a book about mental illness. I loved writing ever since I was little. I remember stapling together big sheets of paper to make books and coloring words and pictures onto the pages. Once I discovered the fantasy genre, I created tales of my own. Some of my early ideas still live within this story.

I never expected to write a book based on two nightmares. You can find more on that after the end of the story. I could explain here, but they spoil parts of the book. Basically, I had two nightmares, my imagination melded them together, and this world came alive in my mind.

I never expected that publishing a book would be so difficult. Specifically, I mean figuring everything out. I dived into the world of self-publishing blind and overconfident. I made numerous mistakes, and

I didn't know what I was doing most of the time. That didn't stop me from quitting. I researched a lot about the book publishing industry and how to improve my craft. I changed my mind constantly about the storyline, even coming up with a new book title and series name. And even while I struggled with mental illness, and believed every day that I would be dead soon from some kind of health problem, I still fought my way through it to work on this book.

I don't know what struggles the future will bring me, but I do know that no matter how dark and unbearable life may seem, even the smallest spark of hope can never be extinguished.

I would like to give special thanks to my editor, Kathy Bosman, for helping to fix tiny errors that I would have never noticed and transforming my previous attempt into a more professional book. Also, thank you to MiblArt for creating the cover and the map that I always dreamed of. And thank you for the title page.

Pronunciation
Guide

Ehckrist – Eh-krist
Hanarthar – Haw-nar-thar
Jayce – Jayse
Landaro – Lan-dar-oh
Lythannen – Lih-than-nen
Roechellar – Roh-shel-lar
Torrannon – Tor-ran-non
Tyringild – Ty-rin-gild
Vendenall – Ven-deh-nall
Wierlling – Weir-ling
Yana – Yaw-na

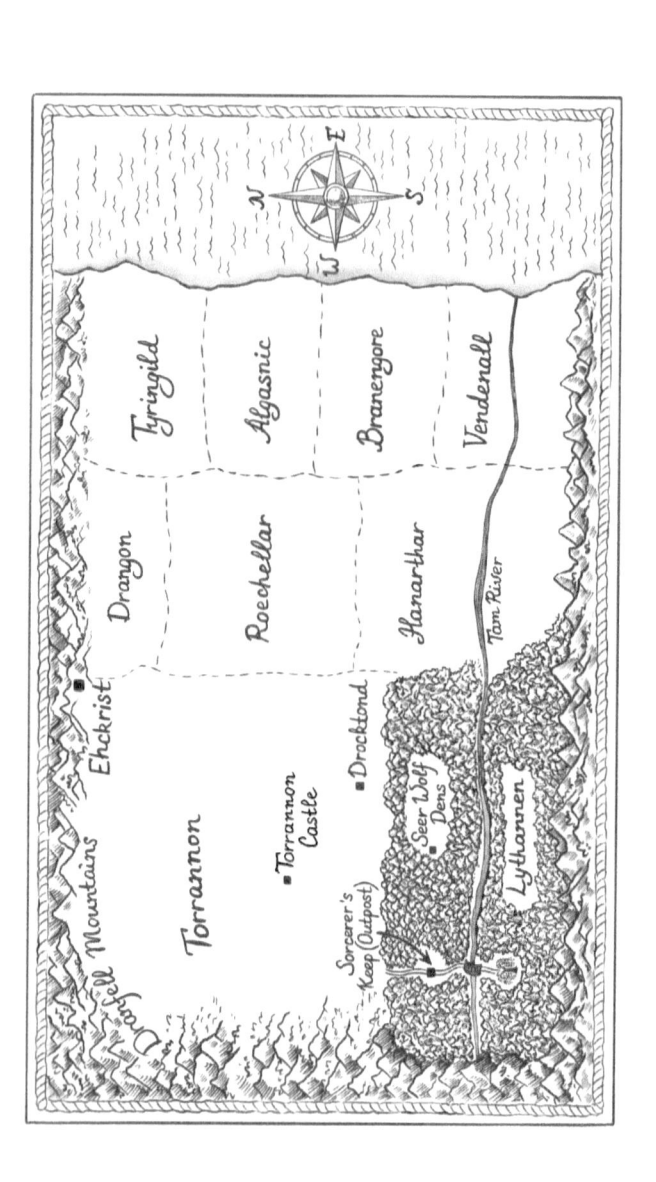

ONE

E VERYTHING WAS WONDERFUL. ACTUALLY, everything was perfect until the day her entire world fell apart.

Aria, the only daughter of King Garne and Queen Amelia, was like any young adult: reckless and with a distinct lack of fear that anything could go wrong. The princess, who had long, wavy, brown hair and hazel eyes, was full of life and loved every minute of her existence. She was destined to one day rule the kingdom of Torrannon. Her life was filled with surety, and her path already lay before her feet.

She lived in a grand castle, constructed out of light gray stone, with a tower on each corner of the lofty keep. A high wall encircled the structure. Villages peppered the lands around the castle except in front of the main entrance.

The vast forest of Lythannen was to the south. To the east were two rows of kingdoms. Drangon, Roechellar, and Hanarthar bordered Torrannon. Tyringild, Algasnic, Branengore, and Vendenall were set along the coast. The Dranfell Mountains encompassed Lythannen and all the kingdoms to the north, west, and south.

One day, Aria's mom fell ill with an unknown ailment. The healers did everything they could to save her, but she died before they diagnosed the cause of her sickness. They suspected intentional poisoning because the illness had suddenly started after she ate, but they never found any proof. The people loved their queen, so no one understood why anyone would harm her. The exact cause of her illness remained a mystery.

Aria's entire world changed. For twenty-four years, she understood the world to be black and white regarding illnesses and health. There was always an obvious way to fix whatever ailed a person because the ailment could always be identified. When they could not be healed, there was a clear-cut reason. She believed no sudden, unknown dangers existed that could bring down a person still so strong and full of life.

Aria had never been an anxious person before—a bit of a worrier at times but never excessively. Now, she didn't know how to be calm and content because if a mystery illness killed her mom, she could suffer the same fate.

She had been sick plenty of times but never seriously. Aria had spent most of her life in blessedly good health. She didn't allow her thoughts to dwell on stories about illnesses and conditions that resulted in death.

Soon after her mom's death, Aria had a panic attack late at night while thinking too much about the possibility of some unknown disease taking her life. She felt a knot in the pit of her stomach, and anxiousness swept rampantly through her body like nothing she had ever experienced before. After she calmed down a little, Aria resolved that if a terrible misfortune should occur, there was probably no way to prevent it. She hoped everything would look better in the morning.

Her resolution was thrown out the window after she woke up to a peculiar sensation. A steady beating rhythm rocked her body. She realized that the sensation was her heartbeat, but she had never been so aware of it. The rhythm wasn't off, yet it was louder than normal.

Her body had betrayed her. She had just said that everything would be better. Apparently, there was more than a mystery illness for her to worry about. Aria didn't want to die right now. This caused a panicked trip to the castle's healers.

"They're called palpitations, and they're a normal response to the panic attack. As long as the rhythm isn't frequently abnormal, even when you aren't anxious, you should be fine. Just relax. Try taking deep breaths when you feel panicky," one of them said.

Aria attempted to use the deep-breathing method whenever anxious thoughts surfaced. Although the technique did help with quieting the panic, the seeds of anxiety had already been planted and grew slowly each day.

The possibility of an abnormal heart rhythm resulted in her continuingly checking her pulse for days. Sometimes the skin on her neck burned from touching it multiple times a day. She never heard anything unusual, and considering that when her heartbeat was loud, the rhythm remained normal, she was pretty sure nothing was wrong.

Her issues with palpitations faded away, but an endless cycle of physical symptoms continued. Excruciating headaches, that made her think she was having an aneurysm, dizziness, that made the room spin, nausea and stomachaches so bad she could barely stand, excessive sweating, and several other sensations all followed.

Aria lost control of her body. When one symptom faded, another swiftly appeared. She couldn't let her guard down for one second because if she couldn't figure out that the sensation was nothing to worry about or caused by anxiety, then it could be the sign of a more nefarious condition.

Panic and imagining the worst possibility became her first instinct rather than rationally analyzing why she was in pain or didn't feel right. Even if she thought nothing was wrong with her body, the anxiety wouldn't always let her trust her own judgment.

She kept thinking that if she went to a healer when she wasn't sure about a symptom and they assured her that nothing was wrong, then she could relax. But this was only a temporary fix. She always felt embarrassed to look as if she was paranoid about everything, so she stopped going unless a symptom seemed too unusual.

Falling asleep took longer than usual. Then, she couldn't stay asleep. Aria spent many frustrating nights waking up multiple times and wishing the sun would hurry and rise already. An increase in nightmares left her wishing she could close her eyes and fall into a state of blissful nothing without any dreams or just not have to sleep at all.

All of this led to exhaustion. She had experienced fatigue before but nothing as intense as this. Her mind ran fine, yet her body had no energy or motivation to do what she asked, even if she slept well. A bone weariness settled over her after any spikes in anxiety. Most of the time, she didn't feel as if she had the strength to leave her bed.

The anxiety wasn't focused exclusively on her health. The fear also bled into her daily life.

Training to wield weapons meant she could die if she made a major blunder, like losing her grip on something because her hands were too sweaty from anxiety. Handling fire could cause any number of catastrophes. Lighting a candle now took twice as long because she didn't want to make a mistake. Visions of falling and breaking her neck flashed in her mind when she walked up or down stairs.

Working among the people meant possible danger if someone tried to hurt her. Plenty of royal guards were always present, but Aria was more watchful and suspicious. Appearing to be calm and in control took a massive and exhaustive effort for her to accomplish.

Every time Aria was alone, her thoughts were hyper-focused on the ever-growing list of everything that could kill her. All the what-ifs piled up in her mind. Any sense of safety in the castle and in her own body disappeared as the fear of the unknown increased.

Darkness washed over her. No matter where she sat, the walls of the world closed in as terror-filled thoughts suffocated her mind. She couldn't fully relax, not when another danger, either real or imagined, always waited around the next corner. Depending on the intensity of the anxiety, deep breathing didn't always help anymore.

With almost every aspect of her life becoming more difficult to deal with because of the anxiety, depression also sprang up. Aria couldn't think clearly anymore, and she was weary of feeling scared almost constantly about something suddenly killing her. She wondered if the people of Torrannon would want a princess who was practically frightened of her own shadow.

She was aware that other people dealt with problems similar to hers, but there wasn't much help for them. Mental illness wasn't a condition people could sleep off, bandage, apply a salve, or take medicine for. Healers offered advice, but they couldn't cure issues of the mind. People just coped with their mental illnesses the best that they could, most of the time in silence.

Opening up about it was difficult because some people never understood what those with mental illness went through. Demands to get over it or relax didn't improve the situation. Causing people to feel ashamed about their mental illness, to supposedly motivate them to get better, was never the best method.

Aria knew one of those speeches would never help her. She would just tumble down deeper into her dark pit, with the added guilt that someone thought she was acting ridiculous for being stuck in an unhappy mindset. Her position of power demanded her to not show weakness and invite negative judgment. It would not be ideal if her people believed she was unfit to lead them even before she became queen.

Anxiety and depression both screamed in Aria's head all day, every day. The fear and the hopelessness had their claws in too deep for her to pull them back out easily. This was no state of mind to be trapped in when one day she would run the kingdom, and the people would depend on her.

Or to live day-to-day life.

TWO

ARIA SAT AT HER desk in her bedroom, pondering about what her life had become while blankly gazing at the night sky out of the two windows in front of her. Silver moonlight and the warm glow of candles lit the room. She had changed into her favorite purple nightgown a little while ago, but her mind was too wound up for her to sleep.

Her bed was to her left with soft, white sheets, a turquoise bedspread, and fluffy pillows. A chest sat at the foot of the bed. A wardrobe was on her right with her clothes, armor, and weapons. A full-length mirror was attached to the wall next to it. To the right of the door behind her was a four-shelf bookcase filled with books. Some of them were for studying, and the others were her own personal collection.

A large rug, with a colorful floral pattern, lay in the middle of the stone floor. Paintings and tapestries of horses, nature scenes, and family portraits decorated the walls. There was also a banner of her kingdom's standard, which was a yellow sunburst motif set on a dark blue background. Her wooden armchair had cushions tied to the seat and the back. Simple and comfortable would best describe the room; however, Aria was anything but comfortable.

She played with her feather-quill pen while staring at a blank page in her leather-bound notebook. Aria liked to write poetry on occasion. She would never say she was highly talented at writing rhymes, but the hobby was enjoyable and used to be stress relieving. Tonight, she had no inspiration. It vanished months ago.

Nighttime was always the worst. Aria only had the quiet darkness to cry out to and her tortured mind to keep her company. Her thoughts, as usual, turned to darker paths.

Over a year and a half had passed since her mom's death. Aria spent every day in agony from grief first and then from mental illness. Even though she remembered what normalcy felt like, waking up and going back to the way she was before seemed impossible now. No joy or light in life existed anymore—only a dark, bottomless pit of fear and misery.

She was sick of always believing that she would die soon. If she had not overreacted about the palpitations, she would never have sent herself down this path. She could have spent so many days happy instead of worrying about everything. All the ways she was so sure she would die always turned out to be nothing or didn't even happen. Aria longed for peace and an escape from this constant waking nightmare.

She turned her attention to the knife that lay next to her on the desk and unsheathed it. No one else was in the room. No one could stop her. The burden of her mental illness would never allow her to one day be an effective queen or to live contentedly.

It would be better if she just ended everything. She had been contemplating this thought far too often lately. Aria never understood before how mental illness drove people to end their lives until her own problems began. Somehow, suicide just turned into the most appealing option to silence the torment.

The emotions warred with each other inside her. The anxiety urged for self-preservation while the depression yearned to take away all the suffering. She couldn't do this. If she did, she would die. But what did she have to live for?

Tears threatened to surface, and her hands shook. She didn't want to die. She was terrified of it. It would be easier, though. No one in Torrannon would miss her.

Aria's breathing quickened. Her chest became tight and painful, and her heart pounded as all the emotions hit her simultaneously. All the worrying about dying would be for nothing if she killed herself right now. But what other choice did she have? She had nothing to live for anymore.

Aria slammed the knife on the desk and nearly tripped over the chair legs in her haste to get away. She collapsed on the bed, covering her wrists with her hands as if trying to protect them from herself.

Aria didn't want to keep living like this. She struggled through each day, trying to hold her fractured mind together. Aria desperately fought back tears. She had spent the past year and a half crying more than she ever had before. Smiling and laughter were rare or forced because she thought everyone would expect her to be happy all the time. Once she was alone, she allowed herself to quit pretending that everything was perfect.

She stayed on the bed for a few more minutes. Her heartbeat and breathing slowed, and her chest stopped burning. The only reason she didn't worry about the chest pain being a heart attack was because she had figured out that it was just an anxiety symptom.

She wiped away the tears that had managed to leak out as her body returned to a calmer state. Aria pushed her dark thoughts away. She didn't know how many more times she would be able to resist before she gave in to them.

Tired and feeling sick, she got off the bed, slid the knife back into its sheath, and blew out the candles. She would try to endure another day. The people would look to her to lead them one day, but all she wanted to do was to go to sleep and never wake up.

Three

ANOTHER RESTLESS NIGHT AND another difficult day passed. Aria was once again exhausted by the time she returned to her bedroom. She dragged her feet as she stepped through the doorway. Then she gasped when she saw someone sitting at her desk. She relaxed after she spotted the Torrannon royal guard uniform.

Each royal guard wore a dark blue cloak, black pants, a dark blue coat emblazoned with a yellow sunburst on the front, and a shirt of chain mail underneath the coat. The cloak and the coat distinguished them from the knights. They only wore more chain mail, leather armor with steel plates, and a steel helmet if the situation called for it. The women in all ranks of the kingdom's army had a choice of whether they wanted to wear a dress as part of their uniform or not.

Aria took a breath and put a hand on her chest. "Jayce, you scared me."

Jayce was her boyfriend. They'd met two years ago after he joined the royal guard. He was charming, kind, a true gentleman, and everything she could have ever imagined.

The green-eyed, brown-haired royal guard with short stubble grinned with amusement. "Then I suppose I shouldn't surprise you like this. I wouldn't exactly be doing my job right if I cause you to die of fright."

"Surprising me is fine. I'd just prefer if you'd do it where I expect you to be."

Jayce pouted. "But that ruins the purpose of a surprise."

Aria smiled and shook her head as he stood and walked over to her. Jayce wrapped his arms around her. She gladly pressed herself up against him and lay her head on his chest.

If everything else was darkness, Jayce was her one beacon of light shining through the gloom. His good-natured and easygoing attitude helped her feel calmer when she was around him. Whether she was the princess or not made no difference to him. He loved her for simply being her.

Jayce had been there when her mom died, offering a shoulder to cry on or providing the comfort of a strong, steady presence to sit quietly with or to talk to. There was never any judgment, only quiet reassurance. He did more for her than she could ever ask and that he even realized.

But she never talked with him about her mental illness. Besides her dad, Jayce was the only person she was close to. She just didn't want to bother either of them with her problems. The time she spent with her dad and her boyfriend was supposed to be happy without her bringing the mood down.

Temporarily forgetting about her mental illness was easy when talking about it might have been wiser.

Jayce and her dad knew a little bit about the anxiety but nothing about the depression. Her trips to the healers were hard to hide from them, and her anxious behaviors weren't always easy to cover up. But they believed that her problems only occurred for brief amounts of time. She didn't have the heart to explain the full extent of her mental illness to them.

Aria imagined conversations with her dad and Jayce, but following through in real life was difficult. She felt guilty to give them a reason to worry about her, especially because her dad had enough on his plate running the kingdom.

Aria also wondered if they might be judgmental about her mental illness. Would her dad still believe that she could handle inheriting the throne? He might think she was weak and useless. Would Jayce still love her? He might break up with her and find a new girlfriend who wouldn't be a burden. The uncertainty left her too scared to risk telling them the truth.

She clung tighter to Jayce. He rested his chin on her head—she only came up to his shoulders in height.

"Is everything all right?" Jayce asked.

He must have felt her tense up.

"Yes." Her response came out more hesitant than she intended.

"Why do I feel like that's not true?" Jayce gently pushed her back.

"I am okay," she repeated in a firmer voice. Aria gave him a fake smile, hoping he would believe her. "I'm just tired."

"Okay." Jayce returned the smile. "You can always talk to me about anything if you need to."

"I know. I need to go to bed now. I have to be up early in the morning."

"I'll see you tomorrow then. Good night. I love you."

"I love you, too. Good night."

Jayce and Aria shared a quick kiss.

After he left, she let out a long sigh and closed her eyes. Jayce deserved someone better to love him.

FOUR

F AR TO THE NORTH and deep in the mountains, another troubled soul watched the sun rise from her perch overlooking a lush forest in the valley below. She slouched where she sat and barely lifted her head to admire the gorgeous vista. She was Landa, a phoenix. The fire bird was the daughter of Landaro, leader of the phoenixes, and Yana, his mate.

The first phoenixes took refuge from a terrible storm in a cave carved into a mountainside in the Dranfell Mountains. They decided to call it home, and their descendants still dwelled there. The phoenixes named the cave Ehckrist, and it was impassable except by flying. Ehckrist was located near the northern border of Drangon and Torrannon.

Phoenixes were proud and noble creatures. They were larger than eagles with long, elegant necks and tail feathers and yellow eyes and beaks. Their bodies were lithe and muscular, and a crest of feathers sat behind their heads. Their plumage was predominately scarlet red with orange-and-yellow markings unique to each phoenix. Rarely, they were solid red. Landa's chest was dappled with orange-and-yellow patches.

Phoenixes possessed the ability to light themselves on fire. Then, with their broad wings, they could cast those flames. Though not immortal, they lived for hundreds of years.

Landa didn't feel proud right now.

Two years ago, she was flying over the lake below the cave. Landa liked letting the tips of her wings and her feet skim the surface, sending cool water droplets spraying through her feathers. Most of the flock were out enjoying the beautiful spring weather.

Landa gazed at her reflection in the water, once again trying to light her feathers. She was the proper age to be able to set herself ablaze. She just needed to keep practicing. While she admired the sparks on her feathers, everything went wrong.

A strong crosswind unexpectedly collided into her, knocking her off balance. Now off course, she panicked and tried to roll back into a glide. Any lift she had disappeared, and she plunged into the lake. All the phoenixes learned how to swim in case they fell into the water. However, Landa's swimming experience was limited, and diving into the icy mountain lake without warning wasn't an ideal situation.

The impact drove the breath from her body and severely disorientated her. The freezing cold water soaked through her feathers and bit at her skin. Landa's lungs burned as she desperately tried to figure out which way was up. She flapped her wings to attempt to propel herself upward.

Landa barely realized that something had grabbed her until her head broke the surface of the water. She gulped in a breath of fresh air and saw brilliant orange-and-yellow streaks on the feathers at the ends of her savior's wings. Those were her father's markings. If he had not swooped in and pulled her from the water as quickly as he did, she might have drowned. Once she was safe on the rocky shore, Landa heard a rebuking voice above her.

"That was a ridiculous display of amateur flying. The fledglings can recover from crosswinds without turning into a sopping heap of feathers."

A few others sniggered in agreement. Her father's withering glare silenced them.

Hot with shame and embarrassment, even though she was shivering, Landa locked her eyes on the ground and didn't dare look up to see who all had judged her so harshly.

"Don't listen to them. It was just an accident," her father said in a gentle tone.

But the other phoenixes were partly right. Landa shouldn't have carelessly lost her concentration and gone for an unexpected swim. If she was going to be the leader one day, she had to hold herself to a higher standard, or she would risk losing the respect of the flock.

The next day, she flew out alone to a secluded spot, away from the water this time. She was scared to make another embarrassing mistake in front of the others. Landa started practicing lighting her feathers but to no avail. She followed the instructions and couldn't manage a spark. The well of shame inside her deepened.

Water never damaged a phoenix's powers, so the accident wasn't the direct cause. A thought crept into her mind that maybe her sudden lack of fire was because she now struggled to believe in herself. She had lain awake for most of the previous night, admonishing herself for all of her errors and shortcomings. Failing to set herself ablaze only added to the pile of self-deprecation that she had already built.

In rare instances, some phoenixes temporarily or permanently lost their fire because of issues not unlike the one she was having. Landa never dreamed that this would happen to her. She trembled as anger and fear joined the shame inside. What if her powers never came back? How could she ever be considered a leader when she couldn't fly correctly or set her feathers on fire?

Her father once killed an evil sorcerer who murdered a phoenix and had been spreading chaos and terror. He had been a young leader at the time, so he earned a great deal of admiration from the flock. Her mother was a beautiful and accomplished phoenix.

Then that left Landa.

Her parents were shocked and worried when she told them what had happened. She expected them to be disappointed in her failure, but they were supportive, as always. They assured her that her fire would return soon.

Landa would have preferred for this to remain a secret, but after too many excuses, especially among phoenixes of her own age, the entire flock figured it out eventually. Her friends and family were understanding but unsure how to help besides giving the same reassurances. Some of the phoenixes looked at her with pity. A few stared at her in disapproval, but they held their tongues.

Those few were enough to destroy what little confidence Landa had left. She became so desperate to prove she could be a worthy member of the flock that she pushed herself to be the best at everything. Nothing short of perfection was acceptable. She trained hard until she was one of the best fliers in the flock.

However, she still solely focused on any errors or faults. Landa yearned for approval from the flock and pursued unachievable, high expectations. She no longer believed she could do anything right, and despite multiple attempts, she was still unable to light her feathers.

"What are you so deep in thought about, my dear?"

Landa nearly jumped out of her skin at the sound of her mother's voice. She hadn't heard her fly over and land beside her.

"Sorry if I startled you," her mother said.

"It's all right." Landa lifted her head and straightened up.

The older phoenix settled down next to Landa. Her mother's orange crest of feathers with yellow tips gleamed in the early morning sunlight. Landa nervously wondered if her mother expected an answer to her question because she had no idea what to tell her.

"Landaro told me that you were an amazing flier today," her mother said instead.

Landa had flown with her father and several others to practice various group formations. They ran drills for different weather and wind conditions and attacks, like a volley of arrows. Landa didn't think her flying had been amazing. She had made several silly mistakes that apparently went unnoticed.

Her mother continued, "If you want to, you could give flying lessons to the fledglings. You would be a splendid teacher."

"If I don't make a fool of myself again."

"Don't be so hard on yourself. Even seasoned flyers make mistakes. Remember when I told you about how your father crashed into a thornbush?"

Landa halfheartedly chuckled.

Her mother recounted the amusing story. "He looked like a porcupine once he pulled himself free. He'd been trying to sneak up on and catch a mouse in the middle of a clearing, but he forgot all about his shadow. He was so determined to catch it and impress me that he didn't pay attention to his surroundings, and it led him straight into the thorn bush. Your father was quite the mess when he was younger."

His accident barely compared to Landa's. Her father's mistake had only been in front of one phoenix, he never lost his fire, and he was still highly respected by the flock.

"Mother, I may fly well, but I can't set my feathers on fire. I'm not even a real phoenix." Her voice faltered at the admission. Landa met her mother's gaze, and the intensity of warmth and love that she saw in it surprised her.

"My daughter, a phoenix never truly loses their fire. Your flames will return. Your father and I believe that, and one day, you will, too. You are worthy to be a phoenix with or without your fire."

FIVE

A RIA ENJOYED SOME DOWNTIME. Her dad gave her the day off, and she planned to spend most of it in the library. She wore a well-worn, comfortable gray shirt and a pair of blue pants rather than a more formal outfit. Jayce took over the duties of one of the other royal guards, who was sick, so she was alone.

Being the crown princess didn't mean she could laze around every day looking pretty. Her dad kept her busy with duties from sunup to sundown. Weapons training, studying, shadowing him, and taking care of small matters, that he thought she could handle by herself, filled her days. If they weren't wasted being anxious about something, she used her free moments to read, write, take care of her horse, Storm, and spend time with Jayce.

Even when Aria wished she could lie in bed all day and sleep until the mental illness magically improved, she didn't have the option. She just had to deal with her issues the best that she could, even when they made carrying out her duties difficult. Aria wasn't keen to ask if taking time off would be acceptable every now and again for fear of sounding selfish. When she became queen, there would be no more days off or as many chances to hide away to deal with the mental illness.

Aria felt mostly calm today and preferred to spend time in her favorite place in the castle rather than locking herself away in her room. Books were of the least concern to her. A bookcase could fall on her, but that was extremely unlikely, considering they were anchored to the walls or to each other. She still sometimes imagined that her own safely anchored bookcase in her bedroom was going to suddenly fall on her.

The library was also peaceful, with not many people present at a time. It was the top floor of the keep, so tall windows on each wall and a skylight in the middle of the ceiling kept the space lit all day.

Aria perused the rows of dark-wood bookcases. The castle's library contained an impressive collection of all kinds of subjects. Unfortunately for her, this included medical knowledge. At one point, Aria constantly leafed through those books to find any ailments that might match her various symptoms.

She quickly realized that researching too much into sicknesses of the body did more harm than good. Aria wasn't a trained healer. Assuming that just one symptom might be the sign of a terrible condition she only read about was too easy. She eventually quit looking and now stayed away from them.

The only medical book that had been helpful was one about different kinds of mental illnesses. Aria found out that her issues with anxiety, specifically heath anxiety, had gone beyond what was considered normal, and after she experienced her first suicidal thought, she realized she was suffering from depression based on the list of symptoms for it.

Her favorite books were fantasy tales—stories that allowed her to imagine being somewhere else safe inside her mind, even if for just an hour. They provided an escape where all of her problems ceased to exist. Aria could pretend to be happy, lost in the stories of other characters' lives before reality slammed back in.

She chose a book and sat in a comfortable, padded leather armchair. As she read, she felt a sensation of being stared at. Aria looked up and thought she glimpsed someone moving away from a dark corner. By the time she stood and went over to get a clearer view, no one was around.

Aria shrugged. It was probably nothing. She returned to her book and dismissed the incident.

Six

L ANDA BLINKED AND SQUINTED when a shaft of bright morning light stung her eyes. Along with numerous cracks and holes, several passages led to the top and the sides of the mountain, so the tunnels in the cave were rarely entirely dark.

A phoenix could always ignite their feathers if they struggled to see. Landa wished she was still able to do that. She never stayed up too late just so she wouldn't have to worry about losing her way in the tunnels at night.

As she stepped forward, a phoenix appeared from around the corner.

"Good morning, Father," Landa said warmly.

"Good morning," he replied. "I'm glad you're awake. I have an important mission for you. The scouts reported that Drangon, Hanarthar, and Roechellar look as though they are gathering their armies for war. They didn't dare to fly too close in case anyone was watching for our patrols. There's no unusual activity in the other kingdoms, so I do not know what Isabel, Bronson, and Rodrick's endgame is. Paying them a visit would be unwise at this point. I can only send one phoenix, so I chose you to investigate this matter thoroughly. You're my best flier. You can sneak in and out without being detected."

Warmth filled Landa's chest at the same time that her stomach dropped. "Surely one of the others will be a better choice. I'm afraid I will mess up or get killed."

"You won't. I know you won't. I trust you to carry out this mission successfully."

Landa took a deep breath to calm her nerves. Her father needed her to do this, and she couldn't let him down. "All right. When do you want me to leave?"

"As soon as you can. Speed may be of the essence."

"I'll go immediately."

Pride glowed in her father's eyes. He laid a wing on Landa's back. "Remember, you don't need to prove anything to me. The failure or success of this mission will not change my opinion of you. You are my daughter, and I love you. I could never think of you as anything less."

"Thank you," Landa said in a tight voice. Shame still swirled inside her. "I just wish I had my fire back."

"You'll get it back. I know the past couple of years have been hard for you, but you should still be proud to be a phoenix."

The words of unconditional love filled Landa with confidence to the tips of her feathers. She could easily mistake the warmth that spread from her chest to her whole body for fire.

Her father followed her to see her off. She heard the familiar trickle of water as they entered the cave mouth. A stream from inside the mountain fell into a shallow pool that the phoenixes used for drinking and bathing.

Her mother waited for them. "Landaro already told me the plan. I know you'll do great, but that won't stop me from worrying about you."

"I'll be back," Landa said. "I promise I will return alive."

"I know, dear. Fly safe."

Landa stepped up to the edge of the cave mouth. She inhaled the crisp mountain air. The sky was clear, and the sun shone brightly. Judging from the slight ripples on the lake and the gentle sway of the trees in the distance, the wind was calm and fair.

Landa spread her wings out. For once since her accident, she felt as if she could accomplish this. She jumped off the edge of the cave mouth.

"May the wind carry you swiftly," her father called to her as she flew away.

SEVEN

FATIGUE WEIGHED LANDA'S WINGS down, but she pressed on. She had investigated Drangon, Roechellar, and Hanarthar over the past six days. It should have only taken four days to fly over the kingdoms and return home, but stormy weather had hindered her progress.

The army of Drangon, led by Queen Isabel, and the army of Hanarthar, led by King Bronson, met in the middle with King Rodrick's army in a remote area in the southern part of Roechellar. The knights traveled through the thickest woods and avoided the roads as much as possible.

Clearly, they didn't want anyone to raise the alarm. Nearly every road in the kingdoms was being patrolled more than usual. No one would pass through unnoticed. Peace among the kingdoms could be tenuous at times, but this was not normal activity for this day and age.

A long time ago, rival groups of humans had created the kingdoms by claiming territory for themselves and defending it at all costs. The rulers were constantly at war, and the lands were plagued by violence and bloodshed. At first, the phoenixes had not concerned themselves with what went on in the world of humans. They watched from afar.

Finally, they could no longer bear to continue to turn a blind eye to the savagery without intervening. Leaving the mountains had become increasingly risky because the humans did not understand at the time that the fire birds meant them no harm. It took years to break negative rumors and superstitions.

Phoenixes had been and still were instrumental in acting as mediators. By sharing their wisdom and desire for peace, they helped the rulers negotiate peace with each other and build a more civilized way of running their kingdoms. The kings and queens were not necessarily allies, but every kingdom flourished ever since those bloody times were left behind.

This was why the preparations for war were so worrying. The rulers were always ready to defend their lands if required, but there hadn't been any large-scale warfare for a long time. It seemed that the long period of peace was about to break.

King Rodrick of Roechellar had been a quiet threat for quite some time. His rise to power came into question after his father died in a supposed hunting accident that was never confirmed by anyone other than Rodrick. There were rumors that he murdered the king to steal the crown for himself. His mother died when he was a child.

Rodrick revealed his immense ambition the moment he took the throne. He increased his army and tried to expand his borders. He claimed his people needed more space to live, grow crops, and raise livestock. A quick look around Roechellar showed an overabundance of food and plenty of uninhabited land. The rulers of the neighboring kingdoms vehemently resisted the expansion attempt until Rodrick conceded. After that incident, the phoenixes kept a closer eye on Roechellar during patrols of the kingdoms.

Landa soared as close as she dared. A thin, foggy layer partially obscured her vision as she flew through the bottom edges of the clouds. Patches of clear sky allowed her to observe the activity below, but she tried to not stay in the open for too long.

She used every technique she knew to fly as smoothly as possible. The more she flapped her wings, the greater the chance that someone would spot her in the open or disturbing the clouds. Landa had no desire to be shot down. If Rodrick, Bronson, and Isabel were so concerned about keeping their armies hidden, they wouldn't be pleased to see that they had attracted the attention of a phoenix.

Landa couldn't hide herself from other keen eyes. When she flew over Drangon a few days ago, a curious peregrine falcon spied her and followed her for a little while. The people of that kingdom fancied the tenacious raptors and used them as a motif on their kingdom's standard, which was a peregrine falcon set on a maroon background.

Landa circled the armies, but she had to stay farther away. She searched for a place to land where no one would notice her dropping out of the sky. Not too far from where the armies were gathered, she spotted high, rocky hills and tall pines interspersed among the other trees. She flew over to the area, dived downward, and safely landed in the crown of a pine tree.

A quick scan of the area revealed that she was alone. The sun had passed its peak and was falling. Landa hunted and rested. At nightfall, she would move in closer.

Landa had to be as graceful and silent as an owl as she swooped from tree to tree. She didn't know where sentries might be posted in the woods. Her mother had taught her this process of sneakily scouting an area from the trees. All phoenixes learned it.

"Move no more than the length of five or six trees at a time," her mother had said. "Reduce the distance if there are more people around. Stop and check your surroundings. Choose your next tree and target limb. Move forward only when you feel safe to do so. The less cover you have, the longer you need to wait and watch."

Flying at night wasn't easy, even though the moon was nearly full. The abundance of spring leaves made picking her next target limb out of the darkness and the thick foliage difficult. Landa's extensive wingspan also tended to excessively rustle the leaves. If she made too much noise, she would freeze and make sure she hadn't caught the attention of anything besides the woodland animals.

Encouraged by her parents' confidence in her, Landa repeatedly told herself, as she had already been doing during the past few days, to try to not become frustrated about errors. Anger would only impair her concentration, and she couldn't risk doing that on such an important mission. Landa cleared her mind and focused on the task at hand. She had trained hard for this. She had the skills. Her parents trusted her, so she needed to trust herself, too.

She halted at the edge of a clearing, hiding in the shadow of a massive oak trunk. Landa estimated that there were over three thousand men and women camping as far as she could see, with armor and weapons sitting around them. Clusters of horses and siege equipment dotted the landscape.

As she observed the alarming scene, three knights approached the tree line and stopped close to her tree. There were two men and one woman. The male knights wore green, long-sleeved shirts, and the female knight wore a long-sleeved, green dress that went down to her knees. They were from Roechellar because the kingdom's standard was an ox motif set on a green background. Landa stayed still and listened intently.

"Does King Rodrick honestly believe that invading Torrannon like this is going to work?" the woman asked in a low voice. "He must know they'll fight to the death to defend their kingdom."

"You know the rumor in Roechellar that King Rodrick ordered for Queen Amelia to be poisoned," one of the men said. "If it's true, I wouldn't be surprised if he's got plans for King Garne and that girl of his. It's a smart strategy. Take out the royal family and you've left a kingdom leaderless and in chaos. No one else would have time to properly take command."

"Do you know when we will be leaving?"

"Now that the other two armies have arrived, I heard we'll leave in the morning and march straight to Torrannon."

The other man glanced over each of his shoulders. "What about the phoenixes?" he asked uneasily, as if he expected one to suddenly appear out of nowhere.

"What about them?"

"Even if we march as stealthily as we can, isn't King Rodrick worried about Landaro's patrols? Surely they'll try to stop us or intervene."

"I don't think the king has ever been concerned about the phoenixes. No one has even seen any recently. We have the element of surprise, and we outnumber Torrannon's army. There's nothing the phoenixes can do to prevent this war."

Landa waited for the knights to leave and quietly retreated far enough to take flight, unseen. The darkness hid her as she hastily soared to Torrannon to warn King Garne. That was the least she could do to help. She hoped any nefarious plots against the royal family remained as rumors.

Eight

Aria yawned as she left her and her dad's private dining room. Today had been a long day of riding to several of the local villages to allow the people to voice any issues or concerns directly to their king. Her dad liked to ensure that their needs were met. He might not be able to help everyone, but he tried his best.

This was just one of the many reasons the citizens of Torrannon admired him, and the same treatment would also be expected from Aria. The food suddenly wasn't sitting right in her stomach as she thought about the big shoes that she would have to fill one day. How would she ever be able to take care of her people when she couldn't properly handle her own mental illness?

"Aria."

She composed herself and faced her dad with a tired and calm expression on her face. Although he was past middle age, and his black hair and short beard were half gray, he still had plenty of strength and life left in him.

"You did a marvelous job today," he said.

"Thank you, Dad." Aria had spent half the time being stuck in anxiety, but she must have hidden it well enough.

"I know you're tired, but there's something I want to ask you quickly." Her dad hesitated. His blue eyes shone with concern. "Are you all right? Is the anxiety better? You never say if you're still having issues."

Aria's heartbeat quickened. She wasn't yet ready to openly discuss her mental illness and its many facets with her dad.

"Yes, I'm doing fine," she lied.

"Ever since your worries over your health began, I've noticed you've been uneasy a lot. I hate seeing you look like, at any moment, something is going to reach out and bite you. If there's anything I can do to help, let me know. I'm your father. If there's any way I can take away suffering from my child, I'll do it."

The compassion in his voice made Aria hold back a torrent of emotions. She desired nothing more than to spill everything and receive whatever comfort he offered her, even though it wouldn't cure the mental illness. But fear made the words die on her tongue. Aria was unsure what to tell him.

"I'll think about it tonight and talk to you in the morning." At least that would give her time to figure out what to say. Maybe he'd get busy and forget.

"All right." Her dad hugged her and kissed the top of her head.

As he walked away, he started up a horrible, hacking coughing fit. He slapped a hand on the wall and leaned against it as he caught his breath and recovered.

"Are you all right?" Aria asked.

"I am," her dad said in a rough voice. "I'm probably just coming down with a cold. A little rest will do me good."

As he left, Aria had flashbacks to when her mom was sick. She had coughed violently after she ate and within hours, blood had come up. After her death, the cooks were careful with the food to make sure it wasn't tampered with. Drinks were also watched carefully. Eating and drinking were two things Aria thought she wouldn't need to worry about at the castle.

A cough wasn't always a cause for concern, but Aria was still worried. She wasn't coughing, so maybe it was just a cold. Aria still decided to keep a close eye on her dad and hoped that the symptom would turn out to be nothing serious.

If he died, she would immediately assume rule over the kingdom, but she wasn't ready to accept the responsibility yet. She could never come to terms with her issues and shoulder the problems of Torrannon and its people at the same time.

Aria felt a tingle on the back of her neck. She whipped her head around, but no one was there. Ever since the incident in the library two weeks ago, from time to time, she had thought someone was watching her. It had only happened a few times, but she felt like a deer being stalked by a hunter. A hunter she could never lay her eyes on.

Aria hurried through the halls to her bedroom. She checked behind her constantly. The cold tingles running down her neck and her back didn't stop until she darted into her room and shut the door. She waited for a few minutes, but it seemed as though no one had followed her.

Aria breathed a sigh of relief. This might just be another anxiety symptom. Maybe she should ask a healer about it tomorrow. For now, she needed to relax and go to sleep.

A strange noise woke Aria up. It sounded as if it had come from inside her room, but that couldn't have been possible. She listened for any more noises but heard nothing else. The night watch and a few staff members would be out and about right now, so Aria assumed that one of them must have made a noise in the hall. Or she'd imagined it.

Aria resisted the urge to punch her bed. It was still dark. She hadn't slept all through the night for several days. She just wanted a full night's rest. Was that too much to ask for? Then she became aware of the whistle of the wind. She looked at her windows. One was open.

Aria groaned. "I thought I closed those."

The window probably hadn't been latched all the way, and the wind opened it. She considered being lazy and leaving it, but there were a few papers sitting on her desk that didn't need to be blown all over the room.

She sighed in annoyance as she dragged herself out of bed. Aria walked over to the window and reached out to pull each sash back together. She stopped when she realized something wasn't right and stretched a hand out to feel the strength of the wind. The gentle breeze wasn't strong enough to pull an improperly latched window open.

She looked down in a panic to determine if it was possible for anyone to climb up to her bedroom. Aria hadn't ever considered the possibility before. In the dark, she couldn't see clearly enough. Her room was two floors from a partially lit walkway below. One lone knight strode past. Otherwise, the area outside was quiet.

Aria closed the window and turned around to scan her room. She could barely see thanks to the cloudy night.

"Jayce, are you in here?"

Nothing stirred.

"If you are in here messing with me, it's not funny. I am so breaking up with you if you think this is a joke."

Aria wished Jayce would have popped out of hiding because that still left her wondering if she was alone or not. She should have taken the feeling of being watched more seriously and discussed her suspicions with her dad, Jayce, or someone else earlier. It was time to leave the room. She would ask one of the royal guards or knights on duty to check. They'd understand.

However, she would be embarrassed if they found that nothing was wrong in the first place.

They might wonder if she was hearing imaginary noises and losing her sanity. Aria ran a shaky hand through her hair. Her anxiety was heightened enough that she would never be able to sleep without reassurance that she wasn't in any real danger.

Problem was, she had to cross the room from the window to the opposite wall. Her bedroom was spacious enough for the door to look as if it was a long way away. She could shout for help, but that might give an intruder time to grab her or cause a big scene if there was no danger in the first place.

She needed a weapon as a precaution. Aria opened a desk drawer and pulled out her knife. She unsheathed the blade and held it at the ready. The same knife she had been thinking about using to end her life might now be her only chance of survival.

Aria stepped briskly toward the door. Anxiety raced uncontrollably through her body, and her chest felt as if it was on fire. When she was a few steps from the door, she spotted movement in her peripherals. She tried to scream for help and get into a defensive stance, but the intruders were too quick.

One of them clamped a hand over her mouth and wrapped an arm around her in a vice-like grip. The other intruder grabbed her right arm and squeezed her wrist painfully enough to force her to release the knife, which they caught so it didn't clatter on the floor.

More moonlight filled the room, and Aria recognized the ginger hair of the one who took her knife to be Karl's—a staff member. He was still wearing his uniform. The one restraining her had short, blond hair and a dark blue coat. He was Everett—one of the royal guards. Aria never expected to be attacked by two people who worked so closely alongside her.

Karl handed her knife to Everett. Aria froze when she felt the blade being pressed against her side. A wave of dizziness hit her. Everett's hand was half blocking her nostrils.

Anxiety threatened to spill over and hinder her ability to think. Aria struggled to not hyperventilate and pass out. She knew the risks of being the crown princess, but she had hoped that she would never be the victim of a traitorous act such as this.

Karl pulled out a small glass flask filled with purple liquid from his pocket. The traitors forced Aria to swallow the concoction, and she lost consciousness.

NINE

J AYCE ROUNDED THE CORNER and witnessed an unusual sight.

"Princess Aria, are you awake?" a maid called. She knocked on Aria's bedroom door. "Princess?"

"What's going on?" Jayce asked.

The maid pursed her lips and wrung her hands. "Princess Aria isn't up yet. She's usually eating breakfast by now. Her father is too sick to leave his bed. I hope she's not in a similar predicament."

"I'll go in." Jayce feared he would also find Aria too ill in bed to get up, but he didn't understand why she wouldn't call for help. He hoped she had just overslept.

"Aria?" Jayce gave her a moment to answer. "I'm coming in."

He didn't expect to walk in and find nothing. The bed was unmade, and a window lay wide open. Jayce took a step forward, and his foot bumped something that made a metallic clang. He picked up Aria's knife from the floor. Jayce put two and two together and rushed to the window.

Something flapped on the edge of the window frame. A tiny piece of purple fabric was caught on the wood. Jayce pulled it off and realized that it was a piece of Aria's nightgown.

"Call the guards," he said to the maid, "and tell Vivian to inform the king that the princess is missing."

Everyone searched the castle, but Aria was nowhere to be found. Her horse was accounted for, but two others were missing. A head count of the castle staff revealed that Karl and Everett were also gone.

Jayce accompanied the captain of the royal guard, Vivian, to update the king on their progress. The middle-aged woman had blue eyes and straight, shoulder-length blond hair. Vivian ran a tight ship and strictly kept the guards under her command in line. Honestly, Jayce was a little scared of the captain to begin with, but he eventually found out that she could be just as gentle and caring.

Jayce held back a gasp when he walked into Garne's bedroom. The king looked half dead. He struggled to sit up. His hair was plastered to his head by sweat, and his skin had a sickly pallor. The only color left was the flush of fever and yellow patches around his eyes. The whites of his eyes also had a yellow tint.

Garne coughed into a handkerchief and sighed dismally when he checked the cloth. Jayce glimpsed a flash of red as the king folded up the handkerchief and set it aside. He felt a twinge of worry. Garne's condition was eerily similar to Amelia's when she had fallen ill.

The king's bedroom resembled Aria's except for a few differences. The bedspread was red, the rug had a colorful geometric pattern, the décor on the walls featured more nature scenes, and there were two wardrobes—one had been Amelia's.

"We cannot find Aria," Vivian said. "Everett, the royal guard, and Karl, one of the staff members, are also missing. No one saw them leave. They slipped out like ghosts, and we can't pick up a trail. Jayce said he found a piece of Aria's nightgown stuck to the frame of one of her bedroom windows and her knife lying on the floor close to the door. We can only assume that Karl and Everett kidnapped her."

"Let me see what you found," the king said in a raspy voice.

Jayce handed him the piece of fabric.

Garne's shoulders fell. "Yes. That's Aria's."

There was a knock, and another royal guard opened the door. "I'm sorry to interrupt. A phoenix just arrived. My lord, she said she must speak with you at once."

"Let her in here," Garne said to Vivian.

The captain found a yellow handkerchief, opened a window, and waved the handkerchief.

The phoenix flew in and landed on the desk. "My name is Landa. I'm sorry if this is a bad time, but I bring grave news. King Garne, you must prepare for war."

The king raised his eyebrows. "What?"

"My father's scouts reported odd activity in Drangon, Hanarthar, and Roechellar. He sent me to confirm their suspicions. I flew as close as I dared and saw armies gathering in Roechellar. They were preparing to leave this morning and are being led by King Rodrick. There are over three thousand, at least. You will have an invasion on your doorstep in about two or three days."

Garne slumped down into his pillows as if he was being crushed by the weight of one catastrophe after another. "I should have known that Rodrick would do this. I've tried to keep peace with him, even after he wanted some of our lands. He's ambitious, but I never imagined he'd resort to brute force."

Jayce felt cold dread in the pit of his stomach. Torrannon only had nine hundred knights.

"What would you have us do?" Vivian asked Garne. "We can send out riders to every village to gather the village guards, but they won't all arrive on time. Even then, the invaders will still outnumber us. Should we try sending messengers to the coastal kingdoms? Perhaps one of the other rulers will help?"

"There are numerous patrols in the way," Landa said. "The chances of a messenger reaching the coastal kingdoms alive are slim. I can return to Ehckrist and send phoenixes to ask the other rulers for help, or we can assist with gathering the village guards."

Garne pushed himself back up and leaned forward with his arms resting on his thighs and his head hanging down. In this position, he looked too frail to be the man who rode hours yesterday without hardly breaking a sweat.

After a few minutes, he straightened up with his shoulders back and his jaw set. "Vivian, choose several riders to travel to villages that can send guards to us in time. Then the riders need to go to the other villages and assemble those forces. I don't want individual groups of village guards to try to fight the invaders. They'll just get slaughtered. Keep a close eye on everyone in the castle. We don't know who else may be working against us. We'll save asking the coastal kingdoms for help as a last resort, since they might not even care to."

"And Aria?" Vivian asked.

Garne ran a hand through his beard, his brow furrowed. "Vivian, go see to the preparations. Jayce and Landa, stay here."

Vivian bowed her head and left.

"Jayce, I know how much you love my daughter," Garne said. "I'm sure you would go to the ends of the world to find her."

"I'm barely restraining myself from leaving right now to look for her," Jayce said.

Garne coughed into the handkerchief again.

"How long have you been ill?" Landa asked the king.

"Since I ate supper last night," he said.

"When did Princess Aria go missing?"

Garne's eyes widened. "Last night."

"I feared something like this would happen. While I was investigating the armies, I overheard three knights from Roechellar talking about a rumor in their kingdom that Rodrick was responsible for your wife being poisoned. Now I wonder if their words were more than gossip."

"I wouldn't be surprised at this point if he's behind everything. I had hoped that this was just a coincidence, but I can't deny it anymore. I'm having the same symptoms that Amelia did, and they started in the exact same way. I have no way to prove that Rodrick is guilty, though. I don't like him, but I can't accuse him of regicide and kidnapping based on a rumor. Karl and Everett are the ones who probably know the truth. I trusted them for three years, and this is what I get in return." Garne hit the bed with a fist and then broke into a coughing fit. It took him a few minutes to get his breath back. "I suspect that they are long gone by now. They certainly knew what they were doing. Both of them had access to the entire castle, our food, and our drinks. But where would they have taken Aria? Why didn't they just poison her, too?"

"I think I know where she is," Jayce said. He was pretty sure the blood drained from his face as the awful memory, that would haunt him forever, sprang into his mind.

"What is it?" Garne asked.

"I had a sister." Jayce struggled to speak past the lump in his throat. "She suffered from mental illness. We visited a village called Drocktond for a festival, but I didn't realize how close it was to Lythannen. She..." Grief and guilt rose up that was so intense, it threatened to overwhelm him.

"Your sister was killed by a wierlling," Landa said for him. "I'm sorry."

Jayce nodded, unable to speak.

"I'm sorry, too," Garne said. "I can't imagine what it's like to lose a loved one that way."

Jayce locked his emotions away. "Aria has been anxious and not acting like herself for over a year. It wouldn't have been difficult for Karl and Everett to notice. The most dangerous place for a person like her would be the sorcerer's keep. If they are planning on killing her, there's a high chance that they took her there. With your permission, I'll go to the sorcerer's keep alone if I have to and see if she's there."

Garne looked as though he was considering the offer carefully. Jayce knew that calling his plan risky would be an understatement. Aria might not be at the sorcerer's keep, but it was the only lead they had that made sense.

Garne finally nodded. Fear for his daughter's life must have overshadowed any misgivings about the rescue mission. "You understand that I would jump on my horse right now and ride with you if I could. I need Vivian here, and I'm reluctant to send a group of knights or royal guards because I don't know how many of them may also be traitors. But I do know I can trust you, Jayce. You'll do everything in your power to bring Aria back safe. You have my permission to leave. Ride out at once."

"Yes, sir."

"Landa, as much as Torrannon needs aid right now, it also requires a strong leader. I need Aria back here in charge, so I'd like for you to go with Jayce. Only phoenix fire can kill a wierlling, so your magic will protect my daughter and this brave young man who I'm sure will be my future son-in-law." The king frowned. "I guess witnessing my daughter's wedding is a future I won't see."

"Maybe we can find an antidote," Jayce said.

Garne shook his head. "We couldn't find a cure for Amelia, and I doubt one would be found right now, either. It's over for me."

"I'll go with Jayce," Landa said. "I know where the sorcerer's keep and the path that leads to it are, so I can guide him."

"Thank you. Jayce, in case I don't get the chance, tell Aria that even if she has issues with anxiety, she will still be a great queen of Torrannon. I love her, and I believe in her. And be careful in that forest. The both of you."

Jayce hurried to pack, stopping in Aria's bedroom to grab gear and clothes for her. He saddled his girlfriend's big, black stallion and his own bay mare, with a white stripe on her face, named Bridgette.

Lythannen was the last place he was inclined to enter after what happened years ago. Jayce sagged against Bridgette as his chest suddenly tightened, and he struggled to keep his breathing steady. The mare bumped his shoulder with her nose as though asking if he was okay. Jayce rubbed her head and waited until he could draw in a deep breath.

He needed to focus on Aria—not his memory of his sister's death. Jayce built up the courage to mount Bridgette. He galloped out of the gate, and Landa soared above him.

It took most of the day to reach Lythannen. Jayce reined in the horses as they reached the edge of the forest. The dirt path in front of him would lead to the sorcerer's keep. The trees around it had been cleared away. The open path and the forest were more like the maw of a beast to him. The densely packed trees and undergrowth harbored deadly adversaries that he knew too well.

When he visited villages near Lythannen with Garne and Aria, he focused on his job and tried to pretend that the forest didn't exist. He never thought he would have to go in it again. As painful memories assaulted him, he found himself frozen in place, unable to convince his legs to squeeze Bridgette back into a canter.

Landa dived down and landed on Storm's saddle. "Are we going in, or do you need a moment?"

Jayce didn't think entering the forest would be this difficult. Fleeing back to the safety of the castle would be easy, but he would never be able to forgive himself if his courage failed him now. He'd lost his sister to this forest. It wasn't taking Aria away, too.

"Let's go," he said.

TEN

ARIA WOKE UP SLUGGISHLY, feeling as if she was trying to swim toward consciousness. The concoction that Karl and Everett forced her to swallow had knocked her out thoroughly. She opened her eyes, but everything spun so much, she quickly shut them.

Raging anxiety from when she was kidnapped still lingered. Aria took deep breaths to try to calm down. Once the anxiety lessened, she could at least hear past the pounding of her heartbeat in her ears.

Still with her eyes closed, Aria used her other senses to find her bearings. The ground was hard, uneven, and warm. From her brief look, she thought she saw blue sky and puffy clouds above her. Birds called to each other intermittently, and trees rustled. Cool wind blew past her, and she felt the warmth of the sun. Aria assumed that she was outside.

She felt well enough to try to open her eyes again. A stone parapet surrounded her in a small circle. Aria slowly sat up, fighting back dizziness. She only saw the sky over the crenels, which could only mean one thing.

"Great," she muttered in exasperation. "Now I'm the stereotypical damsel in distress who's trapped on the top of a tower."

Aria slowly stood. She stumbled over to the chest-high parapet and leaned against it until her legs stopped shaking. The dizzy spell passed, and Aria stood up straight without feeling as if she would pass out.

She took a look at the structure below her. It was aged and had more than a few cracks. Vines snaked up and down the stone, and moss patches mottled the surface. Aria was in the central tower.

Walkways with slate covers extended from either side to two smaller towers with pointed slate roofs. Dirt paths led into the forest to the north and the south. She couldn't see any landmarks from her high vantage point besides mountains far away on the horizon to the south and the west.

The castle sat in a clearing with trees surrounding it in every direction. The evening sun deepened the shadows cast by the thick, overgrown forest, enough that she couldn't see much past the tree line.

"Help!" Aria shouted. "Help! Somebody! Help!"

No one seemed to be around to hear her frantic cries. She couldn't find a door either. Aria looked down and noticed some thick vines that might be able to hold her weight and led all the way to the ground. She pulled on one, only for it to rip off with barely any effort.

"Well, that's no good." Aria threw the vine down.

Would she ever escape alive? Would anybody find her? Was anyone looking for her, or were they happy that the burden was gone?

She leaned her elbows on the parapet and scraped her hands through her hair. Suddenly, every hair on her body seemed to stand up. The forest had gone silent as if every living thing held its breath. Aria looked up and saw a silhouette of a person in dark clothes standing on the edge of the tree line.

Hair blew into her face, obscuring her vision. By the time she grabbed the strands and held them away from her eyes, the figure was gone. A sudden chill ran through her.

It only took a moment for the realization to sink in. The Dranfell Mountains were to the south and the west, she was in an abandoned castle in a vast forest, and a strange, dark figure caused her to have chills.

Aria gasped. "I'm in the sorcerer's keep."

An evil sorcerer once lived in the old outpost in Lythannen and created terrifying creatures called wierllings. No one knew his true identity or where he came from. But everyone who had any type of mental illness knew the warnings to never stray too close to where the sorcerer once dwelled.

Aria was now trapped in the heart of this evil place. She dropped back down out of sight, drew her knees up, and buried her head in her arms. Her dad used to take her with him to villages close to Lythannen, but after she started having problems with anxiety, he stopped bringing her. She knew he was protecting her, but she'd felt ashamed that she couldn't perform all of her duties because of her mental illness. Aria had hoped to deal with the issue eventually—not right now.

"This can't be happening."

Panic overwhelmed her. She sniffled and wiped her eyes on her sleeves. She was going to die. A wierlling would kill her.

"Please, someone help me. I can't do this on my own." She broke down.

The sorcerer created the wierllings to be his guards, kill anyone who irked him, and force others to pay for protection from them, mainly people with mental illness. He seemed to have designed them to have a particular taste for the mentally ill, who were their prey of choice. The creatures were constructed purely from magic and were neither flesh nor blood. It was also said that they had telekinetic powers.

Wierllings fed on people who had mental illness by luring them in unwillingly, and then the person was never seen again. Witnesses reported that the victims appeared to be in a trance-like state while approaching one of the sorcerer's creatures. Some managed to break out of their stupor and try to escape but were still dragged to some unknown place. No remains had ever been found.

Although they usually stayed in the area around the keep, sometimes wierllings roamed because they were no longer under the control of the sorcerer, even traveling as far as the border between Lythannen and Hanarthar. People who had mental illness avoided the entirety of Lythannen if they could. No one desired to be killed by an evil creature in the forest, but accidents still happened. Wierllings also attacked if they felt threatened. People who attempted to stop them from killing someone might suffer the same fate.

As Aria recovered from her breakdown, she realized that she needed to find a way out of this perilous situation by herself, if she could. A rescue attempt would put other people in danger. She wiped her face with her sleeves and tried to come up with a plan.

First, she must escape the top of the keep, but until she figured out how, her only course of action was to stay seated. The parapet would hide her from the wierlling's sight for now. The sounds in the forest had somewhat returned to normal, so maybe the creature had left.

Her anxiety made her question how safe sitting in this spot was. The keep was ancient, so the parapet might crumble if she leaned too heavily on it. Logically, that possibility was unlikely, but she couldn't shake the anxious fantasy. To make herself feel better, Aria scooted forward so her back wasn't touching the parapet.

The floor could be in an equally deteriorated state, even though there was no significant cracking in sight. She'd already walked all over the whole circle of stone, so her chances of falling through were probably slim.

Aria's throat felt raw and dry. She needed water. She wouldn't have minded a spring shower to pass through. Her stomach ached from the panic attack and growled occasionally. She wondered how long she had been asleep. Her head also throbbed painfully.

Aria sighed miserably. She turned her head to the right and traced the pattern of the stones with her eyes. That's when she noticed the irregularity.

She checked again. The brick pattern on the parapet was broken by a protruding rectangle. She crawled over and realized that it was a button. Next to the button was a square block on the floor with a crack all the way around. It looked like a trapdoor. Both had been in the shadow of the parapet because the sun was going down, so she would never have seen them unless she looked close enough.

Aria scooted away from the trapdoor and pressed the button. The door opened inward, revealing a ladder.

"Yes." She grinned.

Aria carefully climbed down. She didn't know how fragile the ladder might be.

"Please don't break. I don't need a broken bone on top of all my other problems."

Aria gripped the rungs tighter as her hands became wet with sweat, and her legs shook. She was glad when her foot came into contact with the stone floor. A lever was mounted on the wall beside the ladder. She pushed it up, and the trapdoor locked back in place.

Aria wiped the sweat and the dust off her hands. "All right, step one to escaping this place is done. Now what?"

The staircase in front of her curved downward and to the right. The red rays of the setting sun shone ominously through arched windows on the left. There were little lanterns attached to the other side of the wall, but she had enough light to see. Aria picked up her skirt and began to descend the flight of stairs.

"Ow!" She had stepped on a loose piece of stone. "I wish I had my boots on."

Aria kicked the piece away and checked her foot to make sure she wasn't bleeding. Another problem she didn't need was an infected wound. She paid more attention to where she placed her feet.

"My day keeps getting better and better," Aria grumbled.

She passed three partially open doors on her way down. They were arched like the windows, which seemed to be the style of the keep. She didn't bother to stop and look in the rooms. Aria wasn't interested in exploring at the moment.

When she reached the ground floor, she cautiously checked her surroundings. Two doorways led to the forest paths, and two others led to the covered walkways. Three windows without glass were set between each doorway and all along the walls of the walkways.

Aria couldn't see any wierllings. The birds weren't as chatty as they were earlier. She didn't know if that was normal or if they sensed that something evil lurked nearby. She strode over to the north-facing doorway. Aria could run, but she most likely wouldn't escape the forest alive.

Nightfall was near. No one had come to rescue her, and wandering around in the forest now was too dangerous. She should have just told her dad about her mental illness last night. No one knew to look for her here. They were probably scouring Torrannon and the neighboring kingdoms, trying to find her.

Icy tendrils prickled up her spine. Aria looked to the left and saw the wierlling on the edge of the tree line again. Before she could react, a maelstrom of anxiety and depression formed inside her mind. The mental illness had never tormented her this intensely before. She held her head in her hands as she tried to control the turmoil of emotions.

A massive wave of anxiety crashed into her first. Everything she feared flashed before her eyes. All the imagined scenarios of dying replayed in her mind. Aria gasped and doubled over. Tears filled her eyes, and her breathing sped up.

Then depression gained supremacy. All the dark thoughts she struggled to keep locked away rushed through her mind like a flood. The hopelessness and frustration at not seeing a livable future drowned her in despair and anguish.

She had nothing left. She had no life outside of her fears. No one was coming for her. They never were in the first place. She wasn't worth the time and effort to rescue. She was a burden. Everyone would be happier if she was gone. She would end her suffering. Her body moved of its own accord, and she approached the wierlling. She would find the peace she had been desperately searching for.

As Aria got closer to the wierlling, details of the creature became more apparent. It was taller than her, with ragged, tattered, black robes that were similar in style to illustrations in books of the sorcerer's clothes. Most of the pale face was hidden behind long, thick, black hair. A decayed-looking nose, and a portion of its forehead, mouth, chin, hollow cheeks, and wispy eyebrows were visible. Its bones protruded sharply, and the skin was speckled with patches of gray. Pinpricks of light reflected off humanlike, black eyes with cloudy, gray rings around the pupils. In her right mind, Aria would never approach this sickly looking creature wreathed in an aura of death.

When she was close enough, the wierlling extended its arm to her. An unspoken message passed between them. All Aria needed to do was take the creature's hand, and everything would be better. She raised her arm.

"No!" someone shouted.

That voice sounded familiar. Aria lowered her arm. The wierlling urgently beckoned to her. Aria took a step back. She wasn't so sure now. This was what she wanted, right? To be free?

The rational part of her mind seized her attention, and her sense of self-preservation kicked back in full force. She was in danger. She had to get away now. The creature's spell broke, and Aria stumbled back. Her stomach churned as the horror of what was happening sank in.

The wierlling lunged forward to grab her. Aria screamed, lost her balance as she attempted to run away, and fell. Hoofbeats thundered behind her, and the wierlling became distracted. Aria heard a screech, and a red blur zoomed over her head.

A phoenix slashed at the wierlling with its beak and talons. The wierlling tried to bat the fire bird away. Finally, it turned tail and fled into the forest, the phoenix in close pursuit.

Aria jumped and yelped in fright when something grabbed her arm.

"It's okay. It's just me."

Jayce stood next to her. He was more scared than she had ever seen him. Sweat ran down his face, and he was breathing as if he had run for hours.

"Come on," he said.

Jayce pulled Aria to her feet. He held his sword out in a defensive position. Aria leaned heavily on him, exhaustion and shock hitting her hard.

The phoenix returned and landed in the grass. "Jayce, the wierlling will be back, maybe with others in tow. We can hide inside the keep. I've been told that they don't go in there."

Jayce helped Aria mount her horse. Storm bent his head around, and she stroked his face.

"Hello, my beautiful boy."

The horse nickered softly and nuzzled her hand with his nose.

Aria gathered her reins with trembling hands. She and Jayce galloped back across the clearing. Her vision darkened, and she hung on tight to the saddle and Storm's mane. She lost consciousness as they rode into the ground floor of the keep.

Eleven

J AYCE WOULD NEVER BE able to describe the emotional punch that struck him when he rounded the corner and saw Aria with a wierlling. Being in the forest put him on edge enough, but the feeling increased tenfold as he relived his past horrors.

After they entered the keep, Jayce stopped Bridgette, sheathed his sword, and dismounted. He caught Aria as she wavered in her saddle and took her in his arms, bridal-style. His heart was still hammering in his chest, but he breathed a sigh of relief that his girlfriend was safe.

"She should rest," Landa said as she landed in a window. "There's probably a bedroom somewhere in this place."

Jayce turned to go up the stairs. A thought bothered him. "Landa, why didn't you burn the wierlling?"

The phoenix looked away and shifted from one foot to the other. "I-I can't."

"Why not?"

"I just can't. Are you going to find somewhere for the princess to rest or stand around forever?"

"Fine. I won't ask." He backed down. Jayce thought he saw a flicker of remorse in Landa's eyes.

"I'll keep watch," she said. "Call me if you need me."

The first room up was a musty-smelling bedroom. A window was on the opposite side of the room with a dresser underneath. A full-length mirror sat to the right of the dresser in the corner. The bed was in the middle of the room against the left wall. There was a wooden armchair and a two-shelf bookcase lined with thick tomes next to the bed on his left. A fireplace was across from the bed on the right side of the room.

Jayce laid Aria on the bed. He was still concerned about why she passed out in the first place. Jayce pressed his fingers against the side of her neck to check her pulse. The rhythm was strong and regular. He watched her chest for a few minutes to make sure she was breathing correctly.

Reassured that his girlfriend wasn't about to die on him, he covered her with his cloak. The bedspread alone looked old and dirty, so he didn't want to tuck Aria into the bed. Jayce went back down to the ground floor to take care of Storm and Bridgette.

He took the saddlebags off and loosened their girth straps. Jayce led the horses out the south-facing doorway so they could munch on the grass just outside the keep. He tied the reins around their necks so they wouldn't trip on them.

Then he noticed a stone trough next to the doorway. It was filled to the brim with crystal-clear water. Even the stones on the inside were spotless. He assumed that the trough must be enchanted to keep the water that it collected clean. There had been no rain today, so it probably also magically prevented evaporation.

"You two can just drink out of that," Jayce said to the horses.

Storm and Bridgette stood quiet and tense. They repeatedly stared in the direction the wierlling ran off to. Jayce petted them and spoke to them soothingly until they lowered their heads to graze. He didn't bother to tie them. The horses wouldn't go far without him and Aria.

Jayce stepped back into the ground floor. He looked around cautiously. Even though Landa claimed they were safe here, he still felt exposed and unprotected.

Jayce stuck his head out of the doorway. "Landa, can you come here?" he called.

The phoenix dived down from the top of the keep. "Is the princess all right?"

"Yeah, she seems fine right now. I don't know how well she'll be when she wakes up, so we shouldn't say anything about her father's condition and the invasion until she recovers enough."

"I agree. She's had a difficult day."

"Have you spotted the wierlling again or any others?"

"No. They're staying away. We'll need to wait until morning to leave. They can sneak up on us too easily in the dark."

Jayce nodded and picked up the saddlebags. "I'm going to go sit with Aria. Let me know when you need a break."

"All right."

Jayce returned to the bedroom and checked on his girlfriend one more time. He dragged the armchair closer to the bed. There were logs in the fireplace that looked fresh, even though they should have decomposed a long time ago. Once again, another magical shortcut. He would get a fire going and then sit watch over Aria.

TWELVE

P HOENIXES HAD THE SHARPEST eyes out of
any creature, including humans. Their other
senses were just as strong. When Landa had entered
King Garne's bedroom, the tension and worry from
everyone were so palpable, they clogged the room.
She could almost taste the sour scent of illness and
the metallic tang of blood before she even landed
on the desk.

Even with these incredible senses, Landa was
pretty sure dozens of wierllings could evade her
at the moment. When she chased the creature off
earlier, she had kept it in her sight, and then it
melted into the shadows as quickly as she could
blink. Navigating the twisted maze of branches was
nearly impossible.

Her father sent patrols to Lythannen once or
twice a month to hunt for wierllings. Landa had
only been on one, but they didn't enter the forest
any farther than the uppermost branches of the
trees. She had been confused at the time, but now
she understood why the patrol didn't search lower.
Crashing into a tangle of branches and breaking a
wing, or worse, would leave a phoenix grounded

and vulnerable to an attack by a wierlling. The sorcerer's creatures despised the fire birds.

The phoenixes endeavored to eradicate them, but the wierllings concealed themselves too well. Although many were destroyed when the sorcerer fell, only a dozen had been killed since then. No one had any idea how many were left.

Landa was honestly surprised that she successfully forced the wierlling to flee earlier, but it wouldn't be fooled a second time. She keenly scanned the tree line.

"Why did I have to be the one to do this?" she asked herself.

When she arrived at the castle in Torrannon, she had expected to deliver her message and return home, not immediately leave to go on a new mission. Her parents would be worried about why she was taking so long to come back to Ehckrist.

She wished she could have turned down King Garne's request. He had looked so hopeful when he said that her magic would be able to protect Jayce and Princess Aria. Landa didn't have the heart to make him feel worse than he already looked by telling him that she had no fire.

Another phoenix would be far more capable, but sending for someone else would have taken at least two days. They couldn't have afforded to wait. At least her presence provided sufficient protection so far.

Landa had no choice but to see this through to the end. If she faced a wierlling again, she would have to fight as hard as she could without the use of her fire and without dying in the process.

Thirteen

A RIA GRADUALLY REGAINED CONSCIOUSNESS. She stayed in the peaceful transition from sleeping to being awake for as long as she could. This was the time that any awareness of reality had yet to catch up, and she existed in a state of ignorant bliss. However, memories slowly crept back in. The events she had hoped were nightmares replayed in her mind.

Aria shot up. She was on a bed in an unfamiliar bedroom. Aria remembered that she must be in the sorcerer's keep. Moonlight streamed in through the window to her left. Tonight, a full moon shone clear and bright. A fire crackled in the fireplace in front of her. Her nose tickled. A thick layer of dust covered everything in the room.

"Aria?"

She looked to her right and saw Jayce standing in the doorway.

"Hey, you doing okay?" he asked.

Aria took a moment to assess herself. Besides hunger, thirst, and a dull headache, she was fine. "Yeah, I'm all right, given the circumstances."

Jayce sat in the armchair next to the bed. "I was worried when you passed out. I wasn't sure what was wrong with you."

"I don't know. Whatever the wierlling did to me, when it had me under its spell, drained me of all my energy. I wasn't in the best physical condition, either. Thanks for getting there when you did. I wouldn't be here otherwise."

"You're welcome." His voice sounded thick with emotion.

Aria felt a pang of guilt. "I'm sorry if seeing me in that situation was difficult."

Jayce shook his head and waved a hand. "Don't worry about it. I'm just glad you're all right."

He pulled out food and water from the saddlebags. Jayce and Aria ate and drank in silence. Her headache faded, and with her hunger sated and her thirst quenched, she could think clearly.

"How long has it been since I was kidnapped?" Aria asked.

"About a day," Jayce said.

"Where's the phoenix? That was a phoenix I saw, right?" Her mind was still a bit scrambled at the time.

"Her name is Landa. She arrived at the castle this morning and accompanied me here. She's keeping watch outside. We'll leave in the morning. I brought clothes for you, by the way." Jayce handed her a pair of saddlebags.

"Thanks."

Aria rummaged through them. She would change in the morning, but she pulled out her socks and her leather boots. Aria never thought she would be so happy to see her boots. No more running around barefoot on crumbling stone.

Aria and Jayce sat in silence. Her boyfriend's posture was stiff, and his shoulders were hunched. Something was bothering him. She suspected he would ask her about why she almost let the wierlling take her, but she wasn't ready to give him an honest answer. Aria slipped on her socks.

"Aria—"

"Let's go exploring." She stepped into her boots.

Jayce raised his eyebrows in surprise. "I thought you would want to rest."

"No. I'm okay now," Aria said a little too quickly. "I'm too wound up to sleep so come on."

As she passed by Jayce, he stood and grabbed her arm. "Aria, we need to talk about what happened."

She glanced toward the door and couldn't meet his eyes. "There's nothing to discuss."

"Aria, you can't avoid the subject forever."

She ducked her head and still refused to look at him. If she met his gaze, she would lose the fragile control that she had over her emotions.

"Please talk to me," Jayce said. "I just want to help you."

Aria peeked up at him. He gave her a pleading look that rivaled the cutest puppy.

"Oh, Jayce." He deserved to know, but this wasn't an easy subject to have a conversation about. "I can't talk about it right now."

She took a step away, and Jayce let her go. Aria dashed up the stairs before he changed his mind.

She poked her head in the next room up. It was a storeroom filled with crates, chests, what used to be food, bottles of wine on shelves, and other odds and ends. Jayce caught up as Aria finished looking.

"Anything interesting in there?" he asked in a casual tone.

"Nothing. Just storage."

The top room was more interesting. Moonlight illuminated it through three large windows. Two tables, that were littered with papers and arcane objects, sat in front of the windows and had a chair pushed under each of them. Old books and scrolls lined bookcases on the right side of the room. A cabinet, with glass doors on the top and solid wood doors on the bottom, was on the left side of the room. Plant pieces, powders, liquids, and animal bones filled glass containers. Lanterns were attached to the walls and hung from the ceiling as part of a chandelier fixture.

There were other objects scattered around, but Aria didn't know what they all were. She reminded herself to not touch anything. She didn't want to curse herself by accident.

Jayce examined one of the lanterns closely. "There are no candles in these. I don't think they were designed for oil either. There's orange powder where a candle would sit."

"Maybe they were lit magically," Aria said. "Who knows what all the sorcerer was capable of?"

"He set up a magic stone trough outside to apparently catch and hold rainwater indefinitely, and the water was perfectly clean. The logs in the fireplace don't burn up or decompose either."

Not everyone who claimed to be able to wield magic was authentic. Some were frauds performing parlor tricks. A few were said to have some degree of power. The sorcerer who used to live here surpassed them all.

Aria went over to the table on the right to investigate a black cloth with arcane symbols painted on it. Three skulls faced each other and were aligned on the points of a triangular-shaped symbol. One was a wolf skull, another was about the same size as the wolf skull but looked more cat-like, and the smallest was a bird skull.

Aria realized what they were; the skulls of the only three magical animals they knew of in these lands. Phoenixes were well known by the kingdoms. Seer wolves received visions and shared their foresight with whomever the visions concerned. Although they tended to be secretive and private, everyone knew it was foolish to reject the advice of a seer wolf. They lived east of the sorcerer's keep in Lythannen.

Panthers were elusive and aloof. No one was sure if they were friends or foes because the majority of the stories about them portrayed them as being mercenaries and murderers. They were normally indifferent to humans. Their power was that they could disappear entirely in the shadows. Even a small patch of shade could conceal a panther.

The sorcerer, who had been determined to become the most powerful one of all, discovered that if he combined the magic of a seer wolf, a phoenix, and a panther, he could gain enormous power. No one had tried the spell again since Landaro killed him and spread the word that anyone who repeated the same act would suffer a worse demise.

"Jayce, I'm pretty sure this bird skull is from a phoenix."

He grimaced. "Do you think Landa knows this is here?"

"What are you two looking at?" The phoenix made an untimely entrance behind them.

Jayce and Aria glanced guiltily at each other.

"I came to check on you both, but the bedroom was empty," Landa said.

The phoenix flew over to a clear spot on the edge of the other table. The orange-and-yellow patches on her chest shimmered in the moonlight. Landa spotted the phoenix skull. "Poor Ember. She was just bringing a message to the wolves when she was shot down." Her eyes flashed with anger. "That sorcerer deserved to burn ten times over for the atrocities he committed. My father was merciful, in my opinion."

Jayce reached for the phoenix skull.

Landa continued, "The skulls were never moved out of fear that they were cursed, just by being touched by that evil man."

Jayce jerked his hand back.

The phoenix had a mischievous glint in her eyes. "I'm not sure if they are cursed or not, but that's why they're still here, along with any other remains. I still wouldn't touch anything."

"Noted," Jayce said. He shoved his hands in his pockets.

Aria suppressed a laugh. "Then this disproves the rumor that phoenixes burst into flames when they die and are reborn in the ashes?"

"I've heard of that, too," Landa said. "When we die, we don't come back to life as a chick. Death is final for us. I'm not sure where that rumor originated from in the first place."

"Also, thanks for saving me from the wierlling."

"No problem."

The horses whinnied. Then several sets of footsteps padded up the stairs. Jayce drew his sword and stepped in front of Aria to shield her. A few seconds later, a gray wolf with yellow eyes stepped through the doorway.

Aria breathed a sigh of relief. She thought the wierlling, being angry that its prey escaped, had decided to go ahead and invade the keep with some friends.

"So, you're the ones causing all the commotion around here," the wolf said.

Jayce sheathed his sword. "Who are you?"

"My name is Arrow. Phase, Haven, I found them," he called over his shoulder.

A dark brown wolf with emerald-green eyes and a sandy-colored wolf with brown eyes joined Arrow.

"This is Phase, and this is our pack leader, Haven." Arrow introduced the dark brown wolf and the sandy-colored wolf, respectively.

"Princess Aria, I presume?" Haven asked. "I've only seen you once, when you were younger, and I had been named the new pack leader."

A memory surfaced from when Aria was a child. She had peered around the corner of a doorway into the throne room and watched the she-wolf talk to her parents. "Yes. I remember. How did you know we were here?"

"This is still our territory, even if this area of the forest is cursed with wierllings. Two of my wolves strayed near the path while they were hunting. They heard horses galloping and observed as you three took refuge inside. I'm surprised that you all stayed."

"I was kidnapped and abandoned here by two traitors to my kingdom. Jayce and Landa came to rescue me. We were forced to wait until morning to leave."

Arrow's eyes glittered with curiosity. "Is a wierlling after one of you?"

"We caught the attention of one." Aria was reluctant to share her personal problems with strangers.

Haven regarded her for a moment. Aria felt as if the wolf's eyes pierced right through her.

"As you may know," Haven said, "once a month, on the day of the full moon, my pack is offered foresight in the form of visions or omens or prophecies. Tonight, we all witnessed the downfall of Torrannon. Rodrick will stop at nothing to seize your kingdom. His greed knows no bounds."

"Rodrick is going to attack Torrannon?" Aria asked.

"Yes," Landa said. "Within the next day or two. My father sent me to investigate armies marching from Drangon and Hanarthar to Roechellar. I learned that the rulers intend to attack your kingdom. Rodrick is leading them, and the armies left this morning."

"We suspected as much when Peak flew in to tell us about what Landaro's scouts discovered," Haven said. "A few of my wolves, who were near those kingdoms, brought alarming reports to me."

"Aria, there's more," Jayce said in a serious tone.

There was a flicker of pain in her chest, and she felt like she was overheating. "What else is wrong?"

"I was waiting until you felt better to tell you. Garne has been poisoned."

"Is he sick like my mom was?" She braced herself for the answer that she knew was coming.

"Yes. Landa overheard a rumor that Rodrick was responsible for your mother being poisoned. We don't know if it was gossip or not. Karl and Everett have disappeared, so we have no way of learning the truth."

"All I care about right now is my dad. He may only have one or two days left."

Aria dropped onto one of the chairs before she collapsed. Her body immediately started cooling down, and she rubbed her chest to try to loosen some of the tension. Aria forced her emotions down so she wouldn't lose her self-control in front of Landa and the seer wolves.

This was too soon. She couldn't take on the responsibility of running the kingdom alone yet. The people would realize how messed up she was. They'd wish that she had died and her dad had lived.

"Perhaps he can be cured," Haven said.

"What do you mean?" Aria asked.

"Phase, you were part of the patrol that discovered it."

"When the sorcerer still dwelled here, he enchanted a weeping willow tree," he said. "Purple roses bloomed that were supposedly imbued with magical healing properties. Lightning destroyed the tree soon after, but we check on it during patrols. A week ago, I witnessed new growth and blossoms. I don't know how, but the tree came back to life. We would fetch one, but the roses are blooming too high off the ground for us to reach."

Haven continued, "Apparently, the sorcerer told a villager that he could heal his sick wife with a magic rose, for a price, of course. I don't know how powerful the flowers are, but they could be King Garne's best chance of survival."

"Where is the tree?" Aria asked. A flicker of excitement ran through her, even though she knew this might turn out to be false hope.

"Take the southern path and cross the bridge. The tree won't be far beyond the Tam River."

"I can go ahead and bring a rose to the king," Landa said.

Haven shook her head. "I wouldn't recommend that. You need to remain here as protection against the wierllings. We'll keep watch tonight so you three can rest."

Aria slouched down in the chair with her head bowed. The world-shattering realization had finally dawned on her. Her mom was poisoned. She was never sick with some mystery illness. All of Aria's fears and struggles since her mom's death had been a lie.

"Aria, are you all right?" Jayce asked.

"I need some time alone."

FOURTEEN

L ANDA, JAYCE, AND THE seer wolves left the room. Aria remained sitting for a few minutes, and then she climbed up to the top of the keep. The night was pleasant, with a soft, cool breeze. Somewhere in the forest, two owls hooted back and forth to each other. Crickets chirped and fireflies flitted about in the clearing below. Besides the fact that evil creatures could be watching her, the scenery was exquisitely beautiful.

She gingerly tested her weight on the parapet until she was sure that it wouldn't topple. Satisfied, she leaned against it, folded her hands together, and looked out over the forest. She didn't care if every wierlling in the forest saw her. At the moment, she was too focused on other matters.

She heard soft thuds as someone climbed up the ladder. Jayce emerged from the trapdoor. Aria turned her gaze back to the horizon. She heard Jayce climb all the way up, and he leaned against the parapet next to her.

Aria knew he might ask again about what was going on with her. Even if she refused, he would keep asking until she told him the truth. Despite her fears of a negative reaction, maybe the time was right to finally say something.

"Jayce, I'm sorry I haven't told you about my mental illness before. You're right. I need to talk about it." She glanced at him, tears welling up in her eyes. He pressed up against her. "I don't want to die. I just want everything to stop. Now I know my mom's death was an intentional poisoning. I had honestly believed she developed a mystery illness, and I was so afraid of getting a similar disease. After my first panic attack and the issues with the palpitations, I started worrying about anything that could kill me. Then I developed depression because I couldn't see an end to the health anxiety. If I knew what had actually happened to my mom, then I wouldn't have lived with so much uncertainty for the past year and a half. Now it's all too late. Even though it was a lie that threw me into my mental illness, I can't just easily return to normal."

Jayce wrapped an arm around her. "You couldn't have known why your mother got sick at the time or predicted everything that you would go through afterward."

"I wish I had," Aria choked out in regret. "The anxiety and the depression have too strong of a grip on me. Every day, out of shame, I hide the mental illness from everyone. This is no way to live. I've almost tried to end my life several times already," she admitted in a quiet voice. "The wierlling used my struggles against me and made me believe it would free me from my suffering."

Jayce looked as if he would be sick. Aria read his reaction as frustration or disgust directed toward her. Her heart already started to break. "If you're mad at me, I'm sorry."

He shook his head. "No, I'm not mad. I understand. I understand better than you know."

Jayce rubbed the back of his neck and leaned his elbows on the parapet. "I probably should have told you this sooner. I had a little sister named Tabitha. I called her Tabi. I guess you could say she was like any normal little girl. Nothing dampened her spirits, even when our father left us. My mom was always busy working in a tavern, so I was frequently taking care of her by myself. We worked odd jobs together to help make ends meet, or Tabi would just tag along and help me in whatever way she could."

Jayce's smile at the good memories turned into a frown. "Then Tabi started uncontrollable habits. She collected flowers in a certain number and avoided stepping on cracks and puddles. When we walked, she kept thinking she saw strange things on the ground and had to go back to investigate, only to find nothing. Or she would look back repeatedly. At night, she thought she saw odd shapes in the shadows. Tabi also struggled with reading. I only knew because she told me she constantly had to reread parts of a story that she thought she had missed. Tabi finally came to me and my mom in tears and told us that something was wrong. Her mind wouldn't stop nagging her about these things, and she would get anxious if she tried to ignore it. We went to a healer, and he said she had obsessive-compulsive disorder. The only advice he gave was for Tabi to try to not give in to her issues and to not let them keep bothering her. We talked it over as a family and came up with a few ideas. My mom or I would hold her hand while walking when she needed one of us to. We thought, by keeping her moving, it would help her break the cycle of stopping frequently. When Tabi saw something, one of us would take a quick look and confirm there was nothing so she could trust ignoring her mind. She would try not to get concerned about the number of flowers she picked and not get too upset about walking on things she didn't want to. We tried so hard, but I'm not sure if our efforts really helped at all. There were probably more issues that she hid from us." He paused.

Aria squeezed his shoulder. A trickle of dread rippled through her as she imagined what the next part of the story could be.

"One day, we rode to the village of Drocktond where a festival was being held," Jayce continued. "The trip was supposed to be a normal outing, but I didn't know Drocktond was so close to Lythannen. I wanted to find an excuse for us to leave, but Tabi had been excited for days to go to the festival. I didn't want to disappoint her, and she deserved to have some fun." Jayce's voice became strained, and his eyes were watery.

Aria struggled to hold back her own tears.

"I made sure she stayed close to me, but at one point, I took my eyes off her for a few minutes. She slipped away from me. When I finally found her, she had already taken a wierlling's hand. I yelled for her, but it was too late. The wierlling pulled Tabi into the forest, and they disappeared. My sister was gone. It was my fault. I ran into the forest, but I couldn't find her. Two village guards convinced me to leave. If they hadn't, I would've searched either until I couldn't go on or the wierlling decided it was hungry for seconds. That's why I tried to get you to talk to me. I can't lose you from mental illness like I lost Tabi." Jayce wiped his eyes.

"I'm sorry about what happened to your sister," Aria said. "I'm sorry for putting you through that ordeal all over again."

"Why would I blame you when none of this is your fault? Just like it wasn't Tabi's fault."

Aria's guilt faded. "The blame doesn't fall on you for your sister's death, either. It's these creatures that don't belong in this world and the sorcerer who created them."

Jayce's eyes were downcast, and he didn't respond. Honestly, if Aria was in his place, she wouldn't forgive herself easily.

"I wish mental illness didn't exist," she said.

Jayce nodded. "I do, too. By the way, Garne told me to tell you that he loves you, and that even with your issues with mental illness, you will still be a great queen. He believes in you, and so do I."

Aria grinned. The wind blew gently through her hair, triggering memories of happier times.

"I remember what life was like before I developed anxiety and depression," she said. "I remember living each day with reckless abandon and sleeping with not a care in the world. I could gallop through a field on Storm and feel safe and free. I never allowed myself to focus on what could go wrong or how a little mistake could lead to death. Most of the time I'm so scared, I don't even want to leave my room. When I watch other people, I wish I could be as happy as they look. I know I don't know their whole stories, but I want to enjoy life like them again without worrying about some terrible misfortune befalling me." Aria stared at the night sky with a frown. "I loved to look at the stars at night. Now, they bring me no comfort. All they look like are tiny points of light suffocating in the darkness."

"But they still shine," Jayce said. "Even if you believe you are suffocating in darkness, your light can never be snuffed out entirely. I guess some of us can have everything wrong and still hide our problems behind smiles and laughs. After Tabi was killed, I was a wreck. I would fake being okay, but I felt nothing. My heart had been ripped out, leaving behind a hole I thought I would never fill. I was so angry with myself, so I put my full focus into training to be a knight so I wouldn't have to think about my sister. I thought I could redeem myself for losing her by spending the rest of my life protecting people. Then, after I moved up the ranks to a royal guard, something extraordinary happened."

Jayce looked at Aria lovingly and took her hands in his. "I met you. I don't know if I can ever forgive myself for Tabi's death, but you showed me there can be light in my life again. You gave me a reason to have hope. You repaired my heart when I believed that it would never be whole again. I want to do the same for you. I want to show you what it's like to enjoy life again. I can't bring Tabi back, but I owe her by making sure I don't lose someone else I love to mental illness. You don't have to fight by yourself anymore. I'm here, and I'm not leaving. We're in this together."

Tears of relief rolled down Aria's cheeks as she embraced her boyfriend. "Thank you. I love you so much."

Jayce wrapped his arms around her tight and kissed her forehead. "I love you, too."

Aria pulled back to kiss him properly. All of her fears of Jayce leaving her because of her mental illness vanished. She would no longer face the rest of her life struggling alone. Aria felt lighter and as if a spark had relit inside her.

FIFTEEN

HAVEN WAITED AT THE bottom of the ladder when Aria and Jayce climbed back down to go to bed.

"Princess Aria, may I speak with you?" the wolf asked.

"Sure." Aria looked at Jayce.

"I'm going to go ahead to the bedroom," he said, and then he went down the stairs.

"I know it must be troubling to have a wierlling after you," Haven said.

Aria was caught off guard. "I never said a wierlling was after me."

Haven gave her a perceptive stare. "I can practically smell your fear and your sadness. You can't lie about how you feel to a wolf."

"How has your pack lived alongside the wierllings for so long?"

The wolf sat and cocked her head thoughtfully. "They don't bother us. Even the mightiest wolf can still suffer from mental illness, but my kind are not their intended prey." Her ears drooped, and her eyes filled with sorrow. "Unfortunately, wierllings are also invulnerable to us. Brave wolves have been lost in attempts to save people from them. I know they stray into the eastern part of the forest, but we rarely see them. They avoid us, and we try to avoid them."

"Will your vision about the fall of my kingdom come true?"

"Our visions are only of what may happen. They are never set in stone, depending on the actions of those involved."

"Like me retrieving a magic rose and escaping the forest without a wierlling killing me?"

"Yes. That could play a significant role in all of this, and there may be a way to fight the wierllings. They feed on humans with mental illness by using their own minds against them, so that's the key to fighting back. If they can't exploit the mental illness, they can't control you."

Aria felt the knot of anxiety in the pit of her stomach. "That won't be easy. The wierlling already overpowered me once."

"I can sense great strength in you. If anyone could face one of those creatures and live, I believe you have a strong chance of succeeding."

Aria smiled. It was nice to know someone else had that much faith in her. "I don't know if I'm overstepping my boundaries, but where do seer wolves receive their visions from? Why give a warning about the fall of my kingdom specifically? I've always wondered."

"I honestly don't know why specific visions are shown to us or exactly where they come from. It's just the way things have always been ever since the first seer wolves gained their powers."

"I don't know if this is right of me to ask either, but I could use the aid of your pack with the invasion."

Haven pricked her ears forward. "What can we do to help?"

"Jayce told me that my father is trying to gather as many village guards as he can, but we can't match the invading armies. We won't win by numbers. I can't predict what Rodrick's reaction will be, but I don't believe Bronson and Isabel will want to go to battle against the seer wolves. If they see your pack and refuse to fight, we can avoid war entirely. Rodrick can't defeat my army by himself."

"That's a good plan. Bronson and Isabel respect us, especially Bronson because Lythannen borders Hanarthar. The seer wolves do not normally fight alongside humans, but I believe we can make an exception this time. I have no desire for the kingdoms to be at war, so I will gather my pack in the morning and lead all who are willing to fight to the castle."

"Thank you. With any luck, no blood will have to be spilled."

Aria returned to the bedroom. Jayce was trying to arrange some old, shabby blankets into a pad on the floor. Landa was nestled in the armchair with a blanket tucked around her.

Jayce looked up. "What did Haven want to talk to you about?"

"That I could fight the wierlling by not letting it turn my mind against me."

He raised an eyebrow skeptically. "Is she sure that will work?"

"It's our best chance of escaping this forest alive. At least we have Landa with us."

Jayce shared an awkward look with the phoenix.

"What's wrong?" Aria asked.

"It's all right," Jayce said to Landa. "You can tell her what you just told me."

"Yeah...about that," the phoenix said. "I have no fire."

Aria almost asked Landa to repeat what she said because she didn't think she had heard her correctly. "How is that possible?"

"Two years ago, I fell into a lake after a crosswind hit me while I was gliding. A few phoenixes thought my accident was ridiculous. I'm going to be the next leader, so I feel like I have to be held to higher standards than the others. I lost my confidence, and I haven't been able to set myself on fire ever since. My parents keep telling me that my fire will come back. I still don't know if I believe them."

"So this will all depend on me." Aria felt as if she had been punched in the stomach.

"At the first sign of trouble, we'll run," Jayce said.

"I can't promise that I'll suddenly regain my fire," Landa added, "but I'll keep any wierllings at bay for as long as I can to give you two time to escape."

"I guess we'll see what happens in the morning," Aria said. She hoped she had the courage to face a wierlling and keep her mind firmly under control.

Her dad's life and the future of her kingdom might depend on it. "I also asked Haven for her help with the invasion. She's going to bring some members of her pack to the castle. Bronson and Isabel respect the seer wolves. I don't think they'll want to fight them willingly."

"I doubt Rodrick will back down so easily," Jayce said.

"If the other two withdraw, he will, too. He can't storm the castle by himself."

Jayce nodded and resumed working on his pad. The blanket he unfolded ripped in half. He stared vacantly at the pile of disintegrating rags.

"Jayce, you can sleep on the bed if you want to," Aria said.

"It's okay. You take the bed."

"I meant that you can share it with me."

"You sure?"

"I know we haven't both slept in the same bed yet, but I always feel better when you're close. I'll sleep easier if I know you're right there beside me."

"As long as you're fine with it." He gathered up the blankets and chucked them into a dresser drawer.

Aria didn't fall asleep immediately. She faced the window, wrapped in her gray cloak. She tried to not toss and turn so she didn't disturb her boyfriend's sleep. Jayce chose the side nearest to the door so that if anything threatened them, it would have to go through him first.

She used to believe that assuming the crown with her issues one day was the hardest challenge in the world. Aria sure was wrong about that. She would take becoming a queen with mental illness over facing a wierlling any day.

Aria squeezed her eyes closed. She eventually fell into an uneasy slumber. Anxiety over what could go wrong plagued her mind. Her dreams were filled with darkness and an indiscernible shape trying to drag her into the gloom.

Sixteen

THEY PREPARED TO SET off in the morning. Aria changed into her gray pants and her green travel dress but decided to not wear her cloak. She strapped on her sword and her knife. Jayce told her earlier that he had left her bow and arrows behind because he was in a hurry, and his arms were full. Arrows wouldn't be much use in this situation anyway.

Aria wiped the dust off the mirror with a blanket and stared at her reflection. She still saw the scared young woman who'd just lost her mom, not someone strong enough to go into a mind battle against a wierlling.

"I have to do this for myself," she said. "I need to prove that I'm capable of handling this and that life is worth living, even with its struggles."

She hastily left the room before her courage failed, and she ended up never being able to walk out the door. Aria met up with the others outside. The wolves waited to bid them farewell, and Landa was preening her feathers. Aria and Jayce mounted their horses when they were ready to leave.

"Good luck," Haven said. "I hope I'll see you all again soon."

The wolves bounded back toward the east. Aria and Jayce asked their horses to trot. Landa flew close above them.

"Are you sure you're ready?" Jayce asked Aria.

"I don't exactly have a choice." She kept her attention fixed on the path ahead.

"Remember, no matter what happens, you won't be in this fight alone."

"I fear this is one fight I will be in alone." Aria asked Storm to trot faster.

As they traveled, they watched carefully for any signs of a wierlling following them.

"Everything goes uncomfortably silent when they're near," Aria said. "You'll get a creepy sensation of something evil watching you." If only riding down this path didn't constantly make her skin crawl.

The horses were similarly on edge and alert. They turned their heads and flicked their ears in the direction of any little noise. A couple of doves were flushed unexpectedly from a patch of tall grass beside the path, causing Storm to throw his head with a frightened whinny.

"Easy, boy. It was only a harmless bird." Aria rubbed and patted his neck until he calmed down.

The rest of the trip to the bridge was otherwise uneventful. The path ended at a small clearing. New shoots hung from the uppermost part of the charred skeleton of a weeping willow. Purple roses, from buds to ones in full bloom, adorned the branches.

"The roses are beautiful," Aria said.

Landa flew up to the crown of the tree. She assessed the roses around her and broke one off with her beak. Landa swooped back down, landed on Aria's shoulder, and handed the flower to her. The rose was in peak bloom.

"Thank you," Aria said.

"You're welcome," Landa replied.

Jayce gathered his reins. "Now we need to run. The faster we get out of this place, the better."

Aria pocketed the rose, and then she noticed that Storm's attention was focused on something to the left. He stood rigid and looked like he was scarcely breathing. The birds and the crickets stopped singing.

Aria followed Storm's line of sight. A chill passed through her, and she was pretty sure her heart froze when she saw what was standing in the clearing.

"Jayce."

The wierlling had found them.

"Aria, I know you don't think you have a choice but you do," Jayce said. "We can try to run. You don't have to face that thing."

"I can try to fight it off again," Landa said.

Aria wished there was another alternative. She really didn't want to do this. The anxiety told her to just run and act like none of this was happening. But she was tired of trying to pretend that nothing was wrong. She had to confront her problems head on.

"Landa, you would be sacrificing your life for nothing. No matter what, the wierlling will hunt us down and kill us before we can leave the forest.

More may join the chase. I have to try the method Haven told me about. It's our only chance to live through this."

Jayce gripped her shoulder. "Aria, please. I can't lose you like this."

Landa jumped to the ground as Aria pulled her boyfriend close and kissed him as if it was the last time.

"You won't."

SEVENTEEN

Aria dismounted and tried to not tremble as she approached the wierlling. She stopped a safe distance away. The evil creature waited. Aria took a deep breath as its spell fell over her mind.

The mental illness screamed so loud she wouldn't have been surprised if her head burst. She gasped as the anxiety and the depression attempted to overwhelm her once again.

"Aria!" Jayce called.

She held a hand out to tell him to stay put. Aria grasped at all of her strength to fight back against the wierlling's spell. When she looked at the creature, it tilted its head and seemed confused.

"You won before, but you can't control me anymore. I don't want to die, and you can't convince me otherwise. Recently, I found out something." Aria glanced back at Jayce with a strained smile. All of her energy was engaged in a massive effort to prevent the wierlling from unraveling her mind. "I'm not as alone as I originally believed I was. I can see a future that is no longer shrouded in darkness."

Her newfound hope washed over her, slowly cracking and chipping away at the wierlling's spell.

Aria's voice grew stronger. "I want to live, even if it means fighting what's inside me for the rest of my life. I know my issues won't go away in a day or a month or even for years. If this means I will eventually serve as a queen with mental illness, I don't care. I'll deal with it. I can't keep letting this rule my life. I'm tired of undeservedly being ashamed of how I feel. I have to take back all of the time I lost, sitting and worrying, and truly live again."

Aria stood tall and powerful. Her own determination and will to live shattered the wierlling's spell. The spark inside rose to a roaring flame.

"I am not your defenseless prey. I am no longer afraid of my mental illness nor am I of you. There are no troubled souls for you to feed on here. Not anymore."

The wierlling stood there motionless, eyeing all of them. Then it let out a ghastly scream. The creature swiped out in Aria's direction, and she was thrown aside with an invisible force. Jayce dismounted and rushed over to help, but he was batted away before he could draw his sword.

The wierlling screamed at them again. Storm and Bridgette spooked and backed off. After making sure she wasn't hurt and didn't hit her head, Aria tried to scramble to her feet, but she couldn't move. It looked as if Jayce was held down magically, too.

Aria had felt proud that, for once, she overcame her mental illness, but she didn't expect the confrontation with the wierlling to end like this.

After suffering through all of her other worries, was this really how she was going to die?

EIGHTEEN

L ANDA FLUTTERED ON THE spot, frantically trying to come up with a plan. Aria and Jayce couldn't run. If she attacked the wierlling, she would be entering a fight to the death that would serve as nothing more than a momentary distraction. She needed her fire. Any other phoenix wouldn't hesitate to burn the creature.

The wierlling turned its attention to Landa. It must have sensed her weakness.

"Landa, forgive yourself for what happened in the past," Aria said. "Forget everyone who criticized you. I worry too that my people won't accept me as a leader with my mental illness, but I know that I can't let it overwhelm me. If I can find my fire again, then so can you. You have to let go of the control your fears and your shame have over you."

The wierlling was nearly upon her, but it hesitated as though it was waiting to see if Landa would fight back.

"A phoenix never truly loses their fire," her mother had said.

Landa had made a mistake, and now she was constantly afraid of what others would think of her. But it only mattered what she thought of herself.

Deep down, she did believe she was worthy, and she should be proud of herself, even with her flaws. Landa closed her eyes as she remembered her father's lesson about how to light her feathers.

"Your fire is your pride and joy," he had said. "Sense the blaze inside you. Fill your very soul with the flames. Set sparks on your feathers. Then, ignite them. Let yourself burn in the glory of a phoenix."

Landa flinched when her whole body tingled. Sparks, that she hadn't seen for far too long, glowed on her feathers. The wierlling backed away.

"I am a phoenix, and I will rise."

Landa screeched as she leaped off the ground. With a mighty flap of her wings, she burst into flames. She dived at the wierlling and enveloped it in phoenix fire.

Aria and Jayce were released from their invisible bonds. The wierlling burned up and exploded into a pile of black dust. Aria ran to Jayce, and they hugged each other tight.

Landa flapped her wings after she landed, and the fire went out in a whoosh. "I did it. I got my fire back. You were right. I just needed to believe in myself again."

"I guess this proves that we are worthy to be the leaders our people expect us to be," Aria said.

"No," Jayce said, "you both were always worthy and just needed help realizing it again."

Aria headed toward her horse. "Let's leave this place. We need to get the rose back to my father."

Jayce and Aria mounted their horses and urged them into a gallop. With the enormous weight of her worries now gone, Landa felt as if she was flying lighter and easier than she ever had.

They safely traveled through the forest without any more wierllings bothering them. After a quick discussion at the edge of Lythannen, they decided that Landa should remain with them to keep an eye out for the invading armies so they wouldn't unexpectedly cross paths. A little after nightfall, they arrived at the castle in Torrannon.

NINETEEN

"**H**ALT! OH, PRINCESS ARIA!" One of the knights recognized her as she and Jayce rode up to the castle entrance.

Some knights opened the gate to let them through. Aria and Jayce dismounted, and stable hands ran over to take care of Storm and Bridgette. Landa landed on the ground.

"Is my father still alive?" Aria asked one of the knights. She could barely stomach the possibility that her dad might have already succumbed to the poison.

"Yes. But from what I've heard, I don't know if he'll survive the night."

"Come on. We need to hurry," Aria said to Jayce and Landa.

The castle was abuzz around them with preparations for war. Swords and spears were being sharpened, bows and arrows were readied, and the castle was being fortified. The night watch was more on edge than usual. Aria and Jayce left a few startled knights and royal guards in their wake as they bolted by.

They didn't stop until they reached her dad's bedroom. Aria froze when she saw how much he had deteriorated. His breathing was labored, and his eyes stared upward sightlessly. Memories of her mom in this condition flooded her mind. Tears filled her eyes.

Isaac, a healer, stood next to the bed. He bowed. "Princess Aria, I'm glad you were found. Your father stopped coughing, and if this follows the same pattern as it did with your mother, then he doesn't have long."

Aria snapped out of her distressing thoughts. "We may have found magic to cure him." She pulled the rose out of her pocket and handed it to the healer. "I assume you can use this in the same way as a regular rose?"

Isaac examined the flower. "Yes, I believe I can. He's too weak to eat the petals, but I can brew a tea with them. I'll be back as quick as I can." He rushed out of the room.

Jayce opened a window to let Landa inside. She swooped in and landed on the chest at the foot of the bed.

"Dad?" Aria sat on the bed and touched her dad's shoulder.

He gazed at her for a long moment before recognition finally sparked in his glazed-over eyes.

"Aria, my dear daughter," he said in a hoarse voice, "I'm so sorry."

"No, no. We've brought back an antidote. You're going to drink some medicine, and you're going to get better." That's what she hoped would happen. Aria didn't know if the magic rose would really heal him or if administering it as tea was the correct way to use it.

Her dad gave her a weak smile. "I should have expected that you would find a cure." He noticed that Landa and Jayce were in the room. "Thank you, the both of you, for finding Aria and bringing her back home alive and well."

When Isaac returned, Aria helped prop her dad up so he could drink the tea. Then they lowered him back onto the bed.

"That's the sweetest medicine I've ever tasted," he said.

"Just rest." Aria covered him with the blankets. She reached under them to hold his hand so he would know she was there.

"Your mother would be so proud of you, and I am very proud of you."

Aria nodded, unable to speak. Tears streamed down her face.

Her dad closed his eyes. His breathing slowed, and for a moment, Aria wasn't certain if it stopped entirely.

"Dad?"

"He's fine," Landa said. "He's just sleeping."

"I hope the rose works," Aria said.

"Regarding the invasion, I could try to mediate, but I don't have a lot of experience."

"We'll figure that out later."

By sunrise, her dad's skin had taken on a healthier appearance, and his breathing was deeper and more relaxed. He looked more at ease. Aria had been too worried to even try to sleep. Jayce sat next to the bed in the armchair and stayed all through the night, even though she told him that he could go to bed. They ate a quick breakfast and waited for an update about the invaders.

"Where did you find this flower?" Isaac asked as he studied the remains of the magic rose at the desk.

"In Lythannen, close to the sorcerer's keep," Aria said. "It came from an enchanted weeping willow tree."

"I wish the rose's ability to bear seeds was intact. If it could be replanted, whatever healing properties this contained would have helped a lot of people."

"I guess the sorcerer only wanted one source so no one else could freely benefit from the magic. To retrieve a rose, you have to run through a gauntlet of wierllings."

There was a quiet knock at the door, and then Vivian came in.

"Is Garne doing okay?" she asked with concern.

Aria nodded. "He should recover."

Vivian looked relieved, and then her expression changed to a serious one. "The scouts reported that the armies will arrive at the castle in about two hours. We need to know what your battle plan is."

Aria was torn between wanting to stay with her dad and needing to oversee preparations for war.

She was also ready to crash into bed. Unfortunately, resting would have to wait until later when they weren't about to be invaded.

"Jayce, open a window for Landa and go with Vivian. I'll come in a moment."

After they left, Aria leaned closer to her dad. "I know you probably can't hear me, but I have to leave. I have a plan to avert the battle, but if it doesn't succeed, I'll defend you and this kingdom to my last breath." As long as the mental illness didn't overwhelm her. Aria kissed his forehead.

"I'll stay with him," Isaac said. "Give me a sword, and I will protect him with my life."

Aria went over to her mom's wardrobe and pulled out a sword. She closed her eyes and swallowed back a sob. This was the first time she had looked at anything in there in a year and a half. Aria took a deep breath and pushed her grief down.

She handed the blade to the healer. "This sword was always more ornamental since we were at peace, but it is still battleworthy."

Isaac bowed his head respectfully. "Thank you, my lady."

Aria also grabbed her dad's sword and set it next to his hand to give him a fighting chance should the worst happen.

TWENTY

Aria passed a balcony on her left, and out of the corner of her eye, she spotted red shapes perched on the railing. Landa spoke excitedly to two other phoenixes. One had an orange crest with yellow tips. The other one with orange-and-yellow markings on its wings noticed her.

"Are you Princess Aria?" the phoenix asked.

"Yes," Aria said.

"My name is Landaro, and this is my mate, Yana. We've come to help you deal with this invasion."

"How did you know?"

"We were nervous when our daughter was gone too long, so we traveled here and learned about what was happening. The phoenixes labored long and hard to build peace among the kingdoms. I refuse to allow our efforts to be torn apart."

"Then you know what we're up against. I don't know if the other rulers will care to listen to you, and three phoenixes will not be enough to turn the tide in our favor."

"Did I say it was just the three of us?" Landaro pointed over the railing with his wing.

Aria approached the edge of the balcony. Her eyes widened, and she sucked in a quick breath of astonishment. Over one hundred phoenixes were stationed on the wall.

"Yeah. I'd say that would help," she said.

"We try to not take sides. Our position as mediators requires us to remain as unbiased as possible, but this situation necessitates battling fire with fire. Whatever happens, we shall be glad to stand beside you."

"When they see all of you, there may be no need for a battle."

"Aria," Jayce called.

She looked over her shoulder. Vivian and several other captains and lieutenants waited for orders. This was her first real battle. A hundred different scenarios resulting in death ran through her head. If the other rulers weren't deterred by the phoenixes and the seer wolves, she would be required to lead her kingdom into war, and everyone's lives depended on her wise decisions.

Her chest hurt, and her stomach knotted up. This was too much. Why did she have to deal with an invasion by herself right now?

Jayce laid a hand on her shoulder. "Hey, it'll be okay. This is one battle you won't be in alone."

Aria squeezed his hand and nodded.

She recalled everything her dad had taught her about defending the castle. "I want the archers on the wall. Do not fire until I give the order. The cavalry and the rest of the knights will assemble and wait in the courtyard. The village guards and the royal guards will stay inside the wall in case the gate and the wall are breached, but they'll be sent out if the forces outside are overwhelmed. I want five of the most trustworthy royal guards to protect my father. Anyone not involved in the battle needs to find safe places to hide. And if anyone else tries to sabotage us, stop them immediately."

"Do you want my flock to stay on the wall, my lady?" Landaro asked.

"Yes. But keep out of sight for now. I'll signal when I want you and the others to show yourselves."

"What will the signal be?"

A flash of red caught Aria's attention. A large phoenix feather lay on the floor. She picked up the plume. "I'll hold this up."

Shouts rang out below. Aria looked to find out what was going on. Then she hurried to the gate with Jayce, Vivian, and the others on her heels. Landaro, Yana, and Landa met them in the courtyard.

"Wolves, my lady," a knight said. "A lot of them."

"I requested their aid. Let them through."

Knights opened the gate, and Aria did not expect to see so many seer wolves filing in. From what she had heard, she thought the pack only consisted of fifty members at most, not at least a hundred.

Haven entered last, panting as hard as the other seer wolves were. "Princess Aria, I'm glad to see you. How is your father?"

"He's doing well now," Aria said. "The rose worked."

"That's great to hear. I wasn't certain if we were going to arrive on time. Where do you want us to assemble?"

"Wait here. When I signal for the phoenixes to appear, I'll want your pack to stand in front of my army."

Aria checked around one more time and then turned to her entourage. "I need to change. Ready my horse."

TWENTY-ONE

B ECAUSE TIME WAS SHORT, a few maids helped
Aria change into her armor. She replaced her
travel clothes with a pair of black pants and a
dark blue, knee-length dress with long sleeves.
Her armor matched what the knights, the royal
guards, and the village guards wore, except the royal
version had more ornamentation.

She slipped on a shirt and a skirt of chain mail.
Pauldrons and vambraces guarded her shoulders
and the upper and lower parts of her arms.
A cuirass, with tassets hanging from the waist,
protected the front of her body, her back, and
her upper thighs. She put on knee-high boots with
greaves attached to protect her shins.

A maid braided her hair back into a bun so it
wouldn't impede her vision, and Aria pinned on her
dark blue cloak. She set her helmet on her desk for
the moment.

After she dismissed the maids, Aria allowed
herself a chance to let out her anxiety. She
collapsed into her armchair and breathed deeply.
Aria wrapped her arms around her middle and
closed her eyes. Would the plan succeed? What

if it ended with the death of everyone, including herself?

"If you can have a showdown with an evil creature and win, then you can confront a few humans," she said, trying to calm herself down.

And she needed to stay hopeful that, with the help of the phoenixes and the seer wolves, there might not even be a battle.

A knock at the door startled her. She straightened up and attempted to look as if she hadn't had a panic attack. "Come in."

Jayce entered and closed the door. "They're here. Are you holding up all right? It's okay if you're not."

Aria appreciated that she could answer him truthfully now without feeling ashamed. "No, I'm barely holding it together. I just need a few minutes to come to terms with everything."

"Come here." Jayce opened his arms.

Aria gladly accepted the hug. "I wish this was easier to deal with."

"You'll be fine. Just believe in yourself like you did back in the forest."

"When I confront the rulers, I want you beside me."

"All right."

Aria pulled away from the hug. "I'll be there in a few minutes. Have Storm waiting for me."

Jayce nodded and left.

Aria strapped her sword and her knife around her waist and her bow and arrows to her back. She donned her helmet and took a steadying breath.

Despite all the odds stacked against her, she must prove to herself that she could bravely and effectively defend her kingdom.

TWENTY-TWO

Aria Looked Out Over the balcony to assess the situation. A legion of cavalry and knights on foot marched upon the castle. Today would end bloody if she couldn't prevent the impending battle.

She hurried to the courtyard. Jayce waited on Bridgette and held Storm's reins. Aria mounted and turned to address her army, the phoenixes, and the seer wolves.

She raised her voice to be heard. Aria hoped they wouldn't hear it shaking. "The cavalry will follow me and fan out in front of the wall. The knights on foot will line up behind them. Haven, your pack can sneak out behind the army."

"We'll divide into groups and hide behind the last line of your knights on foot," Haven said. "When you signal, whoever is in front of us can move aside to let us through."

Aria nodded. "I'm going to talk to Rodrick, Bronson, and Isabel. No one make a threatening move until I say so. If I fail, we will be facing an invasion the likes of which we have not seen for a long time. However, the fierce determination to protect our family, our friends, the people we love, and every citizen is what will bring us victory. We will not allow this kingdom to be destroyed."

Many of the knights and guards nodded and gripped their weapons firmer. Aria took a calming breath and asked Storm to trot. Vivian handed Jayce a banner with Torrannon's standard on it as he passed her, and he rode on Aria's left side. This would let the other rulers know that Aria wanted to talk to them.

After passing through the gate, all she was aware of was the beat of the horses' hooves against the grass and her own heartbeat pounding in her chest. She focused on what she planned to say. This wasn't the time to let the mental illness control her.

The other rulers came forward as expected. Each one was also accompanied by a royal guard member who held a banner. They met in the middle of the space between their armies. The royal guards dropped back and positioned themselves behind the rulers.

King Rodrick and his army wore full steel armor in contrast to the other kingdoms. The long period of peace had rendered steel-plate armor unnecessary, but in Roechellar, they continued crafting it out of tradition.

Aria stayed calm and sat up tall and proud. "King Bronson, King Rodrick, Queen Isabel, to what do I owe this invasion into my kingdom?" She kept her tone and body language casual and unconcerned to hide her nervousness.

"Princess Aria, where is King Garne?" Bronson asked. The even-tempered, burly king had blue eyes, blond hair, and a bushy beard. He rode a cherry bay stallion.

Hanarthar's standard was a bear motif set on a dark purple background. Long ago, his ancestors came over the Dranfell Mountains and brought tales of these powerful and fearsome creatures with them. Based on the stories, Aria never wanted to unexpectedly come face to face with a bear.

"Recovering from an assassination attempt. Someone tried to poison him," Aria said.

Bronson and Isabel both looked stunned. The queen's chocolate palomino mare nervously pawed the ground and sidestepped away a few paces. Isabel gathered her reins and maneuvered her steed back into place next to Rodrick's bay mare.

The queen of Drangon had long, dark brown hair and brown eyes. She was a tough but also compassionate ruler. Her mother was from a faraway kingdom over the ocean that was well known for exporting silk.

Rodrick furrowed his brow and tipped his head to the side. He glanced at the other two rulers.

Isabel narrowed her eyes at him. "Did you know about this?"

"No, I didn't," he said with a blank look on his face.

A moment ago, Aria barely restrained herself from drawing her sword on Rodrick. He was potentially the mastermind behind her family's tragedy and misfortunes. Now, she wasn't so sure. He seemed as shocked as the others to hear the news about her dad. His royal guard didn't seem fazed, but considering the rumor in Roechellar about Aria's mom being poisoned, this wouldn't be unexpected.

Rodrick had short, black hair and a short beard. Brazen and quick-tempered, his gray-blue eyes often held a challenging glint. He never backed down easily from any fight.

"Torrannon is weaker than I expected and ripe for the picking," Rodrick said. "Imagine, my lord and my lady, all of this rich and unspoiled land for our own. We shall be the center of wealth and trade."

Aria's kingdom was vast, but the coastal kingdoms were, and would always be, the center of wealth and trade because all trade passed through them first. Rodrick certainly overestimated his ambitions.

"I'm more curious about what happened to King Garne," Isabel said. She nodded to Aria to explain.

"Thank you, my lady," Aria said. "As all of you know, my mother died after contracting an unknown illness a year and a half ago. Over two days ago, my father fell ill with the same condition, which we now know was poison. Traitors to my kingdom also kidnapped me and left me to die in the wilderness." She wasn't going to discuss the sorcerer's keep and her mental illness with the other rulers.

Rodrick still made no suspicious moves besides surprise. Either he was a fabulous liar or he really didn't know anything about what Aria said. She finally accepted that nothing could be done unless he confessed outright. Accusing him with no proof would be pointless and make her look foolish.

"You both are aware of my warnings," Rodrick said to Bronson and Isabel. "Don't listen to the excuses she is giving to win your sympathy." He gave Aria a smug smile. "She knows that Torrannon does not have the strength to fight all of us."

"Oh, do we not?" Aria held up the phoenix feather. She glanced behind her. The seer wolves ran through openings created by the cavalry and lined up in front of the horses while the phoenixes hopped onto the wall and burst into flames.

Isabel and Bronson glanced nervously at each other. Rodrick's body shrank in on itself, and his eyes darted around at Torrannon's unexpected allies.

"Do you three truly want to go to war?" Aria asked. "Are you willing to stand against the seer wolves and the phoenixes? If you withdraw, we will continue to offer you peace, and this invasion will be forgotten. If you still intend to steal my kingdom, I can promise you that every man, woman, seer wolf, and phoenix will fight to the death to defend Torrannon."

"I will not go to war," Bronson said. "I don't want Hanarthar to become an enemy of the phoenixes and the seer wolves."

"You will stand and fight—not be a coward," Rodrick snapped at him.

Bronson scowled. "You do not rule me. I will not lead my people into a war of pure greed." He rode back to his army.

Isabel glowered at Rodrick. "My kingdom is small and can't afford to be ruined by war. I also won't make it an enemy of the phoenixes and the seer wolves. I can see now that Bronson and I were misled into believing that we were justified in attacking Torrannon. But we were merely a means to an end." She cantered away.

Rodrick stubbornly remained. Aria tightened her hands around her reins.

"This isn't over," Rodrick said in a low voice, his eyes cold and flinty. "One day, these lands will be mine."

"You would be wise to keep peace with us," Aria said calmly. "The phoenixes and the seer wolves will not tolerate an unjust invasion again. I doubt Bronson and Isabel will be so easily convinced either. And if you try to hurt us again, we'll be ready for you."

Whatever way that might be.

Rodrick glared at her for another moment and then departed with a huff.

Aria breathed a sigh of relief and slumped in her saddle. Rodrick wasn't half as scary as a wierlling. She was once again proud that, despite everything, she'd prevailed over her mental illness and successfully defended her kingdom without even raising her sword.

Maybe she was capable of becoming the queen.

TWENTY-THREE

O NCE THE INVADERS WITHDREW, Aria finally relaxed. She ordered scouts to make sure the armies departed from her kingdom and changed out of her armor. Landaro sent a few of his phoenixes to inform the villages and any gathering forces that Torrannon was no longer under threat.

Aria checked on her dad and found him alert and sitting up. Isaac left the room to let them talk in private.

"Vivian informed me that you were able to negotiate with the other rulers," her dad said.

Aria sat on the bed. "Apparently Rodrick used manipulation to gain support for the invasion. Bronson and Isabel also refused to fight the phoenixes and the seer wolves."

"They're more levelheaded and have more common sense than Rodrick. Good job. It's the same course of action I would have taken to prevent war."

"When I told them about the poisonings and me being kidnapped, all three of them looked surprised. Rodrick never gave any indication that he was involved in everything that's happened to us."

Her dad frowned. "It makes me sick that Rodrick could be getting away with murder and kidnapping, but it would just be our word against his right now. The only thing we have to work off of is a rumor. We can't go to war and sacrifice our people if our suspicions are wrong. Your mom would never have allowed it. I don't like it, but we'll have to find more evidence."

Aria nodded in agreement. "Dad, I'm glad you're awake. How are you feeling?"

"I'm on the mend. We could have used one of those roses when Amelia was poisoned."

Aria swallowed nervously, fighting back reluctance to talk to her dad about her mental illness. Retelling her struggles was no easier the second time. "There's something I've been meaning to speak to you about. Ever since Mom died, I've been struggling with health anxiety and depression. Sometimes I feel like I don't even want to keep going."

Her dad raised his eyebrows. "When you say you don't want to keep going, do you mean...?"

Aria nodded and looked away. She was surprised when her dad pulled her into his arms. Aria hesitantly returned the embrace. She was afraid that she was putting him through heartbreak for the second time.

"I'm sorry," she said.

"No. Don't be ashamed, Aria. Never be embarrassed to tell me something like this. I'm glad you told me. We will work through this. Let me know whatever you need to help fight this. I couldn't save Amelia, but I will do anything to save you. I'll be by your side every step of the way."

"Thank you, Dad."

"You're welcome, sweetie."

They released from the hug. Aria felt immense relief flow through her that her dad still loved and accepted her, no matter what.

Spurred on by confidence, she continued, "Sometimes I don't know how I'll ever be the queen and simultaneously deal with the anxiety and the depression. I was so scared that I would lose control of the mental illness in front of the other rulers. It took a huge effort to concentrate on negotiating with them."

"Aria, that is the reason you will be a marvelous queen. Even while struggling with mental illness, you still performed your duty admirably. And don't worry, you shouldn't have to worry about inheriting the throne yet for many years. You'll have time to figure all of this out."

Aria smiled. "I promise I'll never give up as long as you never give up on me. This fight won't be easy. I couldn't do it without you and Jayce."

Her dad smiled warmly in return. "I will always be here for you. Never forget that."

"I won't. I need to go say some goodbyes. I'll be back later."

When she walked into the room earlier, Aria had been terrified that her dad would reject her and be disappointed about her mental illness. Instead, she came back out feeling more content than she had been in over a year. Aria joined Landa, Landaro, and Yana on the balcony.

"Rodrick shouldn't threaten you any time soon," Landaro said. "If he does, you will have my flock's support."

"Thank you."

"And thank you," Yana said. "Landa told us how you helped her find her fire again and that you found yours, too."

"You're welcome, and yes, I did," Aria said.

"Then you are a true phoenix at heart. Farewell and take care."

Landaro and Yana hopped off the rail to take to the skies.

Landa stayed. "What my mother said is true. I know who I am now. If my fire disappears again, it doesn't matter. The others will respect me if I show confidence in myself instead of shame. I'll be a stronger leader one day with that mindset."

"I finally feel like I can live without the shadow of fear and death constantly hanging over me," Aria said. "I see joy and light again. I know I can one day be a great queen of my people too, even with my struggles. I just have to learn how to manage them."

Jayce walked up. He had also changed out of his extra armor. "Are you leaving, Landa?"

"Yes," the phoenix said. "You know, we made a pretty good team. I wouldn't mind another adventure."

"Let's hope for better circumstances next time," Aria said. "But you're welcome to visit whenever."

"Then farewell for now." Landa took off to catch up with her flock.

"Princess Aria?" Haven was behind them. "My pack and I will depart if we are no longer needed."

"Thank you for your aid in this whole mess and for your advice back in the forest," Aria said. "We wouldn't have gotten this far without your wise words."

Haven dipped her head. "It was my pleasure."

Jayce and Aria watched as the castle life returned to normal.

"Jayce, I promise I won't let my mental illness take my life," Aria said. "I'm still going to have rough days and some days when I'll forget I'm not alone, but as long as you and my dad are there for me, I know I'll be all right."

Jayce wrapped an arm around her. "I'll be here. That's one thing you don't need to worry about."

Even though the future was uncertain, Aria allowed herself to enjoy a moment of happiness.

TWENTY-FOUR

L ANDA RACED AHEAD OF the flock as they arrived home. She descended into a glide over the lake, careful this time to anticipate unexpected changes in the wind. She burst into flames with glee and spiraled upward. When she set herself ablaze at the castle, the phoenixes next to her had gaped at her.

Landa evened out and dived downward. She remembered how surprised she was when her parents and the flock had arrived at the castle in Torrannon.

"Mother, Father, why are you and nearly the whole flock here?" she asked as she landed beside them on the railing of a balcony. The rest of the phoenixes were positioning themselves on the wall.

"We came to help," her mother said. "We were afraid something had happened to you when you were gone so long, so we checked here first. The king wasn't able to talk to us, but the captain of the royal guard told us that you delivered your message about the armies and then left with another royal guard to help rescue the princess."

Her father continued, "We realized how dire the situation was and rallied the flock when we returned home."

Vivian must not have told them that Aria was possibly at the sorcerer's keep. One of Landa's parents would have rushed there if they had known. Of course, then she never would have had her breakthrough and regained her powers. Her parents were going to be so surprised.

Landa backed up a few steps. "I have something to show you both. We had to go to the sorcerer's keep to rescue the princess. At one point, I confronted a wierlling and this happened."

Landa concentrated and once again set herself ablaze.

The concerned and alarmed expressions on her parents' faces changed to pride and joy.

"Both of you were right. I never truly lost my fire."

"You put on quite the show there," her father said as she joined her parents in the cave mouth.

"I'm just happy to have my fire and my confidence back."

"Your father and I are so proud of you," her mother said. "You overcame difficult challenges and found a way to believe in yourself again."

"Bursting into flames on the outside is easy," her father said. "Finding that fire on the inside is more difficult than anyone ever realizes."

Landa nodded. "I finally understand that."

She now knew that being a phoenix meant more than setting her feathers on fire. It was having the pride and self-worth to ignite the metaphorical flames within. Perhaps the rumor about phoenixes rising from the ashes originated from this feeling.

Twenty-Five

A RIA TOOK HER PLACE next to her dad.

"Are you ready?" he asked.

"Very much so."

They entered the ballroom side by side. Tonight, two weeks after the near-invasion, the kingdom's citizens celebrated their victory. Aria wore a purple dress with golden flower patterns extending from the skirt to the long, flowy, lace bell sleeves, and purple dress shoes. She even took some extra time to style her hair in a waterfall braid—her mom had taught her how years ago.

Aria hadn't fixed her hair up lately because of exhaustion and a lack of care. She felt in the mood today and always thought the hairstyle looked great with her gold tiara that was adorned with sapphires.

She also had a hairpin made with three phoenix feathers. It was pinned on the back her head, and the feathers hung from short silver chains. The accessory helped her remember Yana's words about her being a true phoenix at heart and why she still fought every day against her mental illness. She had even taken a few minutes to twirl and admire herself in her mirror.

Instead of wasting time with a speech, her dad gestured for the musicians to play, and couples began dancing. Aria smiled when she spotted Jayce walking toward her. He wore a nice, dark blue, short-sleeved tunic with silver lining over a white, long-sleeved shirt, black pants, and black boots.

He held out a hand. "May I have this dance?"

"Of course." Aria took his hand, and they made their way to the middle of the floor.

After a bow and a curtsey, they joined the others in a waltz. As they spun and stepped in unison, tears welled up in Aria's eyes.

Jayce pulled her in close. "Are you okay?"

"Yes, I'm fine. I really am." She wiped away the tears. "I'm not sad. I'm happy. At least for this moment, I'm happy."

They resumed dancing, and the mental illness voices weren't screaming in her head for once. She'd endured a few days of exhaustion while recovering from everything that had happened after she was kidnapped. Otherwise, she tried to stay relaxed.

Aria had kept control of her anxiety today. She let her thoughts go blank and focused on dancing with Jayce. He spun her and dipped her down.

A shadow on the wall outside the ballroom doorway caught her attention. It had long hair and tattered clothes. A wave of panic rolled through her. Had a wierlling followed her to the castle? Then a woman wearing a dress with cutout detailing on the skirt and the sleeves strolled in.

She hid the fear from her face as Jayce lifted her back up. Aria tried to forget the incident and focused again on the bliss she had been experiencing.

The shadow of her mental illness lingered despite all the battles she'd already won. The war was far from over. The depression lurked deep inside her mind, and based on what just happened, the anxiety was always poised to strike.

However, with her dad and Jayce by her side, she could attempt to uncover the person who was buried underneath the mental illness. She could rediscover the beauty and wonder in life instead of focusing on the perils and the horrors.

Aria saw a livable future again. Even though countless battles against her mental illness awaited, she believed that she could fight and win. The flames of hope burned inside her. Even if something else went wrong, she would rise again.

Thank you for reading my story. If it's not too much trouble, I would appreciate it if you left an honest review. Even just one or two lines would suffice. See you in the next story!

Keep reading for a sneak peek of Sparks Shall Rise:
Visions and Illusions

CHAPTER ONE

I N THE CLEARING, A breeze whistled through dying grass stalks and kicked up a cloud of dust. Dead, shriveled leaves and pine needles scraped against each other in the trees. A gust of wind made a shower of them fall to the forest floor. The trees were nearly bare. Even the pine cones were gone.

All the other foliage had withered away, leaving the forest hollow and lifeless. No creature stirred. The air was devoid of any scent besides decay. A shadow fell over the forest as angry storm clouds approached.

A seer wolf named Vision lay under an oak tree. She had white fur and blue eyes.

Vision shut her eyes and ran a paw across the ground. She repeated this several more times, pushing her paw down harder with each scrape. When she opened her eyes, reality blinked back into existence.

Puffy clouds sailed lazily across the sky. Vibrant green leaves and pine needles rustled in the wind like roaring waves. Branches creaked and scratched against each other. Cicadas buzzed. Birds sang their melodies and took off in flurries of feathers.

A squirrel scurried up a beech tree, and a hedgehog nosed through the grass next to a blueberry bush. Vision inhaled the numerous scents of the thriving summertime forest. It was hot, but she was cool enough in the shade where she could feel the wind.

A curious hummingbird fluttered over and hovered in front of her nose. She stayed still so as not to scare it. The little bird studied her for a few moments and then flew to a firebush. She didn't know why her parents had named her Vision when she couldn't always see reality in front of her.

Sometimes seer wolves had issues called mental illness, a word they had learned from the humans. That's what she had right now—she was sure of it. Hallucinations weren't something every wolf experienced.

Vision stood and shook off. She wavered with dizziness. It took her a moment to reorientate her mind and her body. The hallucination had been intense—the type that was harder to break out of and recover from. Luckily, those didn't happen often.

The intensity of the hallucinations varied. She might just see a packmate walking by when no one was there, or part of the forest would morph into a rocky landscape in front of her. A step into dew-covered grass created the illusion of a pond instead of a clearing. Other issues included hearing and smelling things that weren't there.

Running a paw across the ground—to feel the rough scrape of dirt, grass, or stones against her pads—shaking her head, or closing her eyes for a moment normally grounded her back to reality. A sound might also snap her mind out of it.

Earlier, another hallucination ruined her hunt. Vision had been tracking a rabbit. She'd poked her head around some rosemary shrubs and saw what she thought was the rabbit sitting next to a magnolia tree. She crouched and stalked closer and closer. Then she blinked, and her prey disappeared. Twigs cracked behind her, and the real rabbit burst out from the rosemary patch. She never caught it.

Vision yawned. She hadn't slept well last night. Her nap earlier hadn't made a huge difference either. She checked the clearing one more time to make sure it was real. The scene remained beautiful, as it should be. Vision shuddered. She never wanted to see the forest so barren and desolate.

Following a trail, where the seer wolves had trampled the ground down so much that they created a path, she headed back to the dens. She stopped when the trail split into three.

Normally, Vision could practically navigate the forest with her eyes closed. When she and her brother, Thorn, were pups, her parents took them all over the eastern part of Lythannen until they knew every tree and stone like the backs of their paws. Now, it wasn't so easy.

On one occasion, Vision had come to what she thought was a fork in a trail. She blindly went down one of the paths and walked straight into a tree. A sore nose and snout aside, she now sometimes questioned which trails were real and which might be hallucinations. She also had to pay attention to not follow ones created by other animals.

Vision took a breath and scratched each front paw across the ground. She gave herself a few moments to make sure she was thinking clearly. Nothing seemed out of the ordinary.

She stared at the trails and made sure she recognized them. One should lead toward the northern edge of Lythannen and Torrannon beyond it. Another trail should lead south toward the Tam River and the Dranfell Mountains. The last trail should lead east toward the dens as long as she didn't overshoot them and end up in Hanarthar. She especially didn't want to get turned around and go west toward the sorcerer's keep.

Vision scraped her front paws across the ground one more time and inhaled the forest scents. Satisfied that she was present in reality, she took the eastern trail.

Vision, a seer wolf, doesn't always know what is real. As her life falls apart because of hallucinations and derealization, she witnesses an ominous sight at a full-moon ceremony. Or is it another hallucination? Vision will be forced to decide if she still is worthy to be a seer wolf, despite her mental illness, or if her pack is better off without her.

The second book in the *Sparks Shall Rise* epic fantasy series is a tale about learning how to face your struggles and find the hero inside yourself, even when all you want to do is run away. Contains content dealing with hallucinations and derealization.

Read Now

THE
NIGHTMARES
THAT CREATED
REAWAKENED
FLAMES

I was walking through a setting that looked like a mall with friends who I didn't recognize. One of them pointed at a place where they said I could find help for my mental illness. The business looked more like a sinister, dark forest, with barely any light shining through the trees. Suddenly, several humanlike creatures with long, black hair, pale skin, and black clothes ran out. People screamed. Another voice said it was a trick. Those creatures pretend to help, but actually, they go after people who have mental illness and eat their souls. Me and the group of friends turned to run, but for some reason, we had to climb up giant, colorful blocks. Everyone made it up except for me. No one came back to help, and I didn't have the strength to jump up high enough to reach the ledge and pull myself onto the block. Before I woke up, I felt sheer panic that the creatures would find me soon and kill me. I woke up quite frightened. It took me a few minutes to realize that I was no longer in danger. The nightmare bothered me, and the memory has never faded.

I saw a girl standing high up on a wall with no way down. A plain was in front of the wall, and a dense, vast forest stretched out behind it. The wall was higher than the tops of the trees. The girl stood on a walkway and leaned against the parapet. She screamed for help over and over, but no one came. The view zoomed out to show how isolated she was and ended. Once again, the memory of the nightmare stuck with me.

I pondered over the second nightmare. Why was the girl trapped on the wall? Why was it important that she escape? Was she in danger? Was something dangerous in the forest? The scene of checking if a vine would hold her weight flashed into my mind. I wondered if those creatures from the other nightmare lived in the forest. I imagined that this girl was a princess who had mental illness, and she would be killed by one of them if she didn't escape.

The rest of the story slowly revealed itself to me from there.

About the Author

Lindsay McCafferty has been writing since she knew enough words to construct stories. After developing mental illness, she combined her passion with her torment. She hopes the tales and characters in the *Sparks Shall Rise* fantasy series will inspire others to find the courage and determination to rise above their own struggles, even if it seems impossible.

authorlindsaymccafferty.com

facebook.com/authorlindsaymccafferty

instagram.com/authorlindsaymccafferty

x.com/lindsaymauthor